AN ECLIPSE OF EVIDENCE

KRISTEN KING

Silvester & Eve Publishing

CONTENTS

Jo's Waning Moon Self-Care Bath

O nce the moon begins to wane and grow dark, take some time to wash away any stress with a self-care bath. First, gather the following ingredients:

2 Tbsp lavender flowers
2 Tbsp jasmine blossoms
1 Tbsp sage leaves, crushed

Pour your ingredients into a small tea sachet as you recite the words:

With these herbs, I let stress melt away. With this bath, I let comfort be the way.

Draw a bath with warm to hot water and add:

1/2 cup powdered coconut milk

Drop the tea sachet into the bath and allow to steep while the bath water runs. Soak in the tub for about ten minutes while closing your eyes and tapping into the nurturing spirit of the moon to comfort you.

CHAPTER 1

The fire crackled in the hearth room as five sets of eyes peered at the shadowed moon stamp on Sorcha Ross Allan's letter. Autumn ran her hand over the stamp, squinting at it curiously. Tavish looked up at her from his place on her lap, as if to give her a questioning look.

"Well, Tav, if you're asking what our first step should be, then I think it's to head home for dinner and magic practice." Autumn scratched the orange tabby cat's head with her other hand and placed the letter down on the table in the hearth room of Parchment and Pine, the girls' paper shop.

"Oh, that's right!" Simone shouted at her cousin from the other side of the fireplace as she slapped the thigh of her black skinny jeans. "I completely forgot that we're supposed to be meeting everyone at Mom's house tonight for practice. We've gotta go."

Lainy, the girls' recently discovered relative who was now a part of their coven, sighed with recollection. "Yeah, I guess your mothers wouldn't be too pleased with us if we were late. I've got my car here, so I'll just meet you both over there. But . . ." Lainy pointed at the letter sitting on the table. The lunar eclipse stamp glistened in the fire's light and sent a chill up her spine. "That letter won't solve itself. If Sorcha's sister is missing, the time for action is now."

James ran a hand through his thick brown hair and nodded in agreement with Lainy. "My mother's coming back this evening, so we can talk with her about what's really going on tomorrow. I don't wanna waste any time either, but it's probably best if we all sleep on it. I know I'll think more clearly with a good night's sleep."

Autumn lifted out of the wingback chair as Tavish jumped to the floor. She wrapped her arms around James and whispered into his ear, "Don't worry. We'll figure out what's going on and find your aunt." She pulled back and smiled at him, smoothing her hand across his stubble beard.

"I know. If there's anyone I have confidence in, it's you." James brushed the auburn locks away from Autumn's eye and turned to look around the room, nodding at Lainy and Simone. "All right, well, I'm gonna head out. You all enjoy your coven meeting tonight, and I'll bring my mother over as soon as she returns." James kissed Autumn softly and headed toward the front door.

Simone pulled the heavy curtains open for him to leave and then made her way to the front window. "The moon's already up. It's a waning gibbous tonight, which means Mom's gone home early from the bath shop to relax before our coven meeting. I can smell the chamomile tea brewing from here, and she's definitely expecting us."

"Well"—Lainy raised her arms up at her sides in question—"what do you have to do to close up the shop? Just put me to work so we can get out of here."

Autumn and Simone gave each other a sly smile. "We've actually been doing a little magic practice of our own here at the shop. Shall we show her?" Autumn pointed to a stack of messy journals thrown around the shelf of a tall hutch on the wall. She lifted her right hand and whispered under her breath, "Turn chaos right. Fix the mess within my sight."

With a swirl of her hand, the books elevated from their place on the hutch shelf and aligned themselves neatly in a row with their covers all visible. Autumn smiled with pride at her handiwork, and Tavish circled around her ankles, shaking his tail with delight at his witch.

"Okay, so practical magic, then. I like it." Lainy nodded and walked back toward the hearth room. "I'll snuff out the fire along with all the candles around the shop."

Simone called to her from behind the shop counter. "That would be amazing, thanks! I'm just gonna turn off the computer and put an energy shield around the shop for the night. There've been some weird energies looming around the mountain region lately, and I wanna maintain the good vibes in the shop."

Autumn stopped organizing the shop for a moment to eye her cousin. "You've been feeling some strange energies? Why didn't you say anything?"

Simone brushed her hand through the air. "It's nothing. I mean, after all that we've been through lately with you almost being killed and all the disruptions with the founding families, I didn't think it was that big of a deal." She shrugged and turned off the computer for the night. "Besides, it's really just around the edges of town that I've been feeling it. Main Street has been pretty normal in terms of energy, but I wanna do the shield just in case."

"Since when are you a just-in-case kind of person? Something's definitely going on." Autumn raised her eyebrows and exchanged a glance with Lainy.

"Tell us what it feels like so we can keep an eye out, too." Lainy threw her camel-colored wool peacoat and black leather gloves on as she spoke. "I mean, I know you're the one who sees auras and senses unseen energies, but maybe since we're all getting closer in the coven, we can sense something, too." She scooped her long brown hair out from under her coat collar and clapped her hands together. "Let's try. It is magic practice night, after all."

Autumn nodded in agreement. "That's right, cuz. What are you always telling me? You don't have to do anything alone. We're right here with you, so tell us how we can help with this energy shield for starters."

Simone twisted her lips to the side and squinted at the two of them. "Yeah, okay. You can help me put the energy shield up for the night. Come to the center of the shop." She walked between the shop tables as Autumn and Lainy followed her with Tavish underfoot. With a quick exhale, she spread her feet shoulder width apart and lifted her chin. "Tune into the energy surrounding the shop. See if you can sense the vibration." She stared straight ahead, across the shop, and through the darkness of the front window. "What do you feel?"

Autumn shook her head beside her cousin. "The quiet street." She stood silently beside the girls for a moment as Tavish rubbed his head against her leg. "There is something, though, in the distance. My mind is telling me it's there, but I only feel it faintly. It seems out of my grasp, but not necessarily a bad energy."

"That's it. The something you feel waits in the mountain region, and I've sensed it as a deep, dense purple moving slowly over the lands."

Lainy tilted her head at Simone. "Purple? As in royalty?"

Simone shook her head and lifted her right hand to shoulder height. "No, more like power, dominance, and strong magic." She began moving her hand in a clockwise motion around her head as she continued. "By my hand, set this protective shield in motion. Let no negative energy pass, only good intentions. Keep this shop and all within it safe and sound throughout the night and beyond the morning's light. With the power of three, so shall it be."

Autumn and Lainy raised their hands and followed Simone's lead by chanting two more times. "With the power of three, so shall it be."

The girls watched as tiny sparkles of golden light shimmered around the outer walls of the shop. Simone nodded with approval and turned to face the girls.

"Right, job done. Now we can go home for some real magic practice and a chat about that letter." Simone pointed to the back room. "I'm gonna grab my things and meet you by the back door."

"Sounds good. I'll see you both at your mothers' house in a minute." Lainy made her way to the front door with Autumn following behind her. She grabbed her leather tote bag and slung it over her shoulder. "I'm eager to hear if Jo's heard anything from Sorcha about her sister. See you in a bit."

Autumn propped the front door open for Lainy and smiled. "Yep, we'll be there." She gave Lainy a wave and locked the door for the night, flipping the sign to read Closed. With a sigh, Autumn glanced around the shop and called back to Simone. "I don't like this uneasy feeling I'm getting. We just got back to normal after clearing all the black magic out of town, and now Sorcha's sister is missing. Plus, you're telling me there's a dark-purple cloud looming in the distance. That sounds wonderful." Autumn walked to the back of the shop and turned off all the lights before grabbing her coat and scooping Tavish up under her arm.

Simone rolled her eyes as she pulled the back door open onto the alley behind the shop. "Autumn, I know as an air witch you're used to knowing what lies ahead all the time, but come on. Now that you're the new four-points witch, we're in unfamiliar territory. This has opened up a whole new can of worms with magical possibilities far beyond what either of us is used to. We'll deal with it all as a coven, but you're gonna have to come to terms with not always knowing what lies ahead. And that uneasy feeling may be more frequent now."

Autumn snuggled Tavish into her face and kissed his head before putting him onto the back seat of Simone's Jeep SUV. "You're right. I know I need to get used to this feeling, but it's a big transition for me. These past few months have taught me that even though my gifts are stronger than ever, I need to stay on my toes. I won't have all the answers every time I'm looking for them."

They both slid into the car, and Simone drove them away from the center of town toward her mother's house. "I just worry that you put so much pressure on yourself to know what's coming and take care of everything, that's all. Give yourself some leeway. No one expects you to know everything and take care of everything, okay? Don't expect that of yourself either. If something's out there, we'll find it. And if something has happened to Sorcha's sister, we'll figure it out, one way or another."

Simone pulled the car into the driveway of Crescent House, Jo and Penny's home, and sat staring at the front porch for a moment. Autumn swallowed hard. "Do you think Aunt Jo already heard that Ayla Ross is missing?"

Dipping her head down to track the waning moon from the windshield, Simone shrugged. "Doubtful . . . But if I know my mother at all, she already felt it through that moon tonight."

CHAPTER 2

T he wafting smell of vegetable noodle soup made its way through the hallway toward Autumn's nose as she removed her boots on the entryway bench. Simone closed her eyes and took in the aroma as well as she pulled off her black quilted coat.

"We're here!" Simone yelled to the kitchen.

Jo came quickly out of the back, wiping her hands on the apron tied around her waist. "Oh, thank goodness! If Lainy hadn't come in a few minutes ago and told us you were on the way, we'd have thought the worst! Come inside and grab a bowl of soup before we're all much older."

Eve peeked out of the kitchen and waved. "Long time no see! I brought everyone's favorite pastries tonight, but really

I'm just hoping to hear the latest scoop." Eve smiled eagerly as Autumn, Simone, and Tavish made their way into the kitchen.

Penny walked over to give her daughter, Autumn, a hug. "Hello, dear. It sounds like you've had another eventful afternoon." Penny raised her hand in Lainy's direction. "Lainy mentioned James came into the shop with a letter."

Autumn sighed as she made her way to the stove, ladling some soup into a bowl. She wrapped her hands around it to warm them and brought it to the kitchen island, where she lifted herself onto a stool. "Yeah, he did. It's from Sorcha, and I've got it in my backpack for you all to see, but it doesn't sound good."

Jo folded her arms around her chest. "It's her sister, Ayla, isn't it?"

Simone and Autumn exchanged looks. "She's missing, Mom," Simone said with a soft tone.

Jo nodded, and a tear formed in her eye. "I felt it as I did my moon ritual this evening. As usual, I went down to the river with my tea and scrying bowl and hoped to receive a vision before you all came over tonight. As soon as I scooped the water into the bowl, I knew an emptiness surrounded the Allan family, and my heart sank."

"What did you see in the bowl, Aunt Jo?" Autumn looked up from her soup to wait for a reply.

Jo wrung her hands together and looked around the kitchen to find her tea mug. "Oh, my dears. A shadow has been cast over Ayla's place in their family . . . one I cannot see beyond.

I kept getting a glimpse of her land on the outskirts of town, but it seemed desolate and distant. It was so unlike the welcoming place I've been to many times." She took a sip of her chamomile tea and stared down at the kitchen island.

"Sorcha wrote the letter that James brought into the Pine." Autumn looked around the room at the coven listening intently to her. "It just mentioned that she had gone to visit her sister as usual but couldn't find Ayla anywhere. I could tell Sorcha had a lot of fear when writing to us. It came through on the page."

"There was a strange ink stamp on the top of the letter, too," Simone interjected as she slid onto a kitchen stool with her own soup bowl. "We figured it was probably a symbol for their family, but we weren't sure."

Lainy nodded and looked directly at Jo. "If I'm not mistaken, it's a symbol for the lunar eclipse, like the one we had the other night." She turned toward Autumn. "Can I grab the letter out of your bag?"

"Oh, yeah, please. It's in the entryway on the bench." Autumn looked at Lainy appreciatively as she scooped Tavish up onto her lap.

Eve put her hands on her hips and eyed everyone with questions. "So Sorcha's sister just vanished out of thin air? Are we sure she didn't just go somewhere without telling anyone?"

"I mean, it's possible." Simone slurped her soup and gave a low groan at how good it was. "But Sorcha's letter mentioned she goes out there to visit her sister all the time. So why would she have left if her sister was coming to visit?"

Lainy walked in with the letter in hand and placed it on the kitchen island for everyone to see. "Here it is."

Penny leaned in closer to read it aloud. "Girls, I have a predicament, and I know I can count on you once again. I went to see my sister for our regular get-togethers. When I got there, she was nowhere to be found. I'm so worried, as I've waited for several days now with no trace of her."

Eve's eyes widened. "That doesn't sound like she just went out for the day."

Penny shook her head and continued. "I thought you could help before I go to the authorities, seeing as how you've been so good with other recent events. Since I haven't been able to get a hold of you lately, I had James deliver this letter. I'll be back in town in a couple days to meet and discuss in person." Penny pointed to the stamp at the top of the letter. "And there's the ink stamp. I'd wager Lainy's right. It is a lunar eclipse."

Jo moved in toward the letter. "Yes, it's like the eclipse we just had. The shadow overtaking the moon. That isn't a symbol I've seen equated with their family before, though. The Allan family has a strong water energy, but it mostly manifests with dreamwork. I know Ayla likes to work with astral projection during certain moons, however. Perhaps something went haywire during one of her out-of-body experiences."

"That sounds tricky." Simone tilted her head back at the thought. "Maybe she lost the cord connecting her with her physical body here. You think she went missing in some weird astral sense?"

"No, that can't be." Penny shook her head and paced the room. "If she were astral projecting, her body would still be here somewhere. It wouldn't be missing along with her spirit."

"Wow, this is beyond my capabilities." Lainy poured herself a cup of chamomile tea and walked over to give Tavish a rub. "Sounds like a lot of water energy and maybe some earth energy mixed in on this one. I don't know if I'm gonna be much help on the fire element side of things."

"We don't know what we're dealing with yet." Autumn put her hand on Lainy's shoulder. "So let's all put our heads together. A full coven is an effective coven, and I get the sense that's going to be my new motto." She looked around at each of them and sighed. "Just please promise me, all of you, that you'll keep your eyes and ears open. This one's gonna take some puzzle-piecing together, so keep your senses heightened and your gifts at the ready."

Jo spoke up abruptly. "I agree. There's something lurking in the shadows here, and that concerns me for the Allan family, especially after her brother, Dillon, almost drowned recently. They've been through a lot already, and this puzzle may take a while to resolve."

Simone bit her lip and looked over at Autumn. "Well, we better keep up with our magic, then, while we wait for Sorcha to return with more details. What's on the docket for tonight?"

Penny pushed the letter to the middle of the kitchen island and looked around the room. "Since we're on the topic of disappearances, I was thinking cloaking spells were in order."

"That's an interesting idea." Autumn placed her dishes in the sink and thought for a moment. "Simone has been trying some energy shields around the shop, and she showed Lainy and me how to do it earlier."

"Yeah, that's true. I guess that's pretty similar to putting a cloaking shield up, right?" Simone shrugged and deferred to Penny.

"It is. You're right." Penny nodded and rubbed her palms together. "Shielding spells are quite similar to cloaking spells. The key lies in preparing a barrier based on your intention." She grasped her hands, swirling them in a circular motion. Opening them, she revealed a line of tiny evergreen trees standing within the palm of her left hand. "In order to create the effect you desire for your spell, you may need all elements to work together. This is where our practice comes in."

The girls all stared at Penny's palm in amazement at the beautiful little forest she'd created in her hand. Jo smiled at her sister as she placed her tea mug down on the counter. She slid her finger along Penny's palm, lifting the line of evergreen trees onto her own finger and placing them carefully along the edge of her tea mug. Dipping her middle finger into the tea, Jo created ripples in the hot water behind the trees.

"Yes, and if you cloak your intention properly," Jo said. "Within your boundary, you can create ripples to change the outcome of any situation." As she spoke, she lifted her gaze to meet Autumn's eyes and within them, Jo glimpsed a familiar but long-lost light capable of overtaking any shadow.

The Edison bulb lights strung up high from the trees in Jo and Penny's garden cast a soft light on the outdoor space. Autumn looked out to the edge of the backyard where the swaying branches of the trees cast shadows over the grounds. The air remained brisk around them as Jo and Penny directed the girls together in a tight circle toward the center of the garden.

"Hey, Autumn." Eve turned to face the girls beside her. "I know it's silly and we might not be out here for very long, but remember that weather-warming spell you did for the founder's dinner a couple months ago? Do you think you could warm the garden for us while we practice?"

"Oh, yeah!" Simone nodded in agreement with Eve as she wrapped her chunky black knit sweater tightly around her hands. "Let's get that spell going again to keep us warm."

Tavish pushed his way through the cat flap on the back garden door and trotted over to Autumn as if frustrated to be left inside. He meowed up at her from beside her feet.

"All right, I guess Tavish is weighing in, too, now. I'll warm us up." Autumn closed her eyes and took a deep breath. She lifted the palms of her hands at her sides and whispered, "Air and fire within me, merge. Flow with warmth and comfort to give this garden the feel of a spring day. Flow with warmth. Flow with comfort." She raised her arms to shoulder height now as the warmth grew within her hands. The winds swirled around her and then died down as a gentle warmth came over the garden. Opening her eyes, she found her mother smiling in front of her.

Penny nodded in approval while removing the shawl from her shoulders. "Very good, my little ladybug. The air and fire within you are a beautiful combination."

"Yeah, thanks, Autumn!" Eve gave her a massive grin as she took her toggle coat off. "That's much better! Now we can really concentrate on our spell work."

"Remember, girls," Aunt Jo said with a serious tone, "you won't always have ideal conditions to perform your spells. Sometimes you'll need them in dire circumstances, and you must still be at your best. So it's good to practice while things aren't perfect. For example . . ." Jo smiled at Penny beside her.

Simone followed her mother's eyes to Penny and then over to the side of the house where a long vine crept up the outer wall toward an outlet. With one quick pull, the vine wrapped itself around the cord for the Edison lights and yanked it out of the outlet, leaving the entire garden dark.

"Whoa, Aunt Penny, that was creepy!" Simone exclaimed.

Jo and Penny chuckled at Simone's remark, and Jo stepped forward to lay her hands on Simone's shoulders in the dark garden. "The darkness is one circumstance you must learn to overcome. Work together to achieve your intentions by starting with this simple obstacle." She strolled around them in the dark as she continued. "Bring your focus and intention to the forefront and ensure you are all in alignment. We'll start with a cloaking spell. Autumn, as our four-points witch, you take the lead." Jo stepped back to stand beside Penny and watch the girls.

"Okay, a cloaking spell." Autumn felt Tavish brush up against her leg for support. She cleared her mind, and Lainy's fire energy immediately came to mind. Turning to Lainy at her side, Autumn perked up. "Let's first give ourselves an advantage of some light. On my count, we'll ignite a flame within our hands. One by the elements surrounding us. Two by the landscape providing for us. Three by the fire lying within us." Autumn and Lainy rubbed their palms together and felt the warmth sparking into tiny flames within their hands.

Lainy opened her palms to reveal the bright flames within them to the others. "Fire to guide us."

Autumn laughed and opened her own hands to reveal another flame. "A pair of flames to guide water and earth to work their magic."

Simone nodded and stepped in closer. "What do you want us to do?"

Lifting the flame toward her face, Autumn looked between Eve and Simone. "Combine the protection of earth along with the clearing of water. I'll say the words, and Lainy will keep the fires going while both of you draw the boundary around us, okay?"

"Yep, got it." Eve put her hand on Simone's forearm to signal her to move closer. The two of them stood back-to-back in the center of the garden and waited for Autumn's cue.

Bringing her flame to Lainy's hand, Autumn carefully dipped hers to the side, allowing the flame to combine into Lainy's. She brought her hands to her mouth and gently blew into them to extinguish the heat. Then, she moved her focus toward the garden as Tavish stomped the ground with pride beside her.

"Elements within us and surrounding us, protect us from outside eyes and ears. Conceal us with the energy of a thick forest, mounted to the sky. Only the rising sun shall reveal what lies within." Autumn walked over to Eve and Simone and placed her hands on both of their shoulders. "With the protection of earth and the clearing nature of water, we draw a boundary around this garden." Autumn dropped her hands from their shoulders, and Simone took that as her cue to continue.

Drawing a large circular motion with her flattened right hand, Simone moved her arm around in a clockwise motion. "Water sweeps away all awareness that is not our own."

Feeling Simone's movements behind her, Eve followed with a circular motion of her own arm. She chanted, "Earth blocks all knowing besides that of our own." The girls circled their arms around themselves three times before standing still once more.

"By the power of three, so shall it be." Autumn finished the spell and blew out a long breath that swooped across the garden in an instant.

Lainy moved toward the perimeter by the trees, holding up the flame in her palm as she walked. "Did it work?" She tried to sense some kind of barrier along the tree line but could not feel anything.

Penny met Lainy at the trees and drew a vertical line in the air with her finger. "A door for one, an opening for none." Penny smiled at Lainy. "Let's test it out, shall we?" Pressing her palm firmly onto the invisible line, she revealed shimmers of golden light around an energetic doorway in front of her. She moved her body through the shimmers and onto the other side of what appeared to be a magical barrier. She gently closed the golden door behind her and motioned in the air to proceed. "Lainy, say something on the other side."

Lainy turned back to see Jo in the center shadows of the garden. Nodding in approval, Jo smiled. "Go ahead. Test it out."

As her excitement grew with the possibility of a successful spell, Lainy's eyes widened and her focus sat on the golden door. "Flames burn bright on the inside. Can you see the light?"

Penny stood on the other side of the shimmering door, waiting for some kind of response but hearing none. She moved a few paces left and right before Jo came to meet her at the shimmering doorway.

"Penny, come back through, dear." Jo pressed her palm firmly against the shimmering door, allowing her sister to walk back into the garden with all of them. When inside, Jo pulled the boundary door back together, sealing it shut with her hand once again.

Eve rushed up toward them. "That was incredible! Could you really not hear or see anything on the other side, Penny?"

Laughing at Eve's amazement, Penny grabbed her hands and looked into her eyes. "You did an amazing job, Eve. All of you did, and I didn't see or hear one thing on the other side of that boundary."

Autumn folded her arms around her chest and shook her head in slight disbelief as she walked the garden. She looked over the lightly shimmering wall lining the edge of the trees. "We did it. Our coven did it!"

Aunt Jo raised her arms and motioned for them all to gather at the center of the garden. "Yes, you did, and I'm very proud of you for accomplishing that. But . . ." Jo glanced at Penny before continuing. "The spell took far too long to cast. If you truly needed a cloaking spell, you may only have seconds to perform it. Consider how you might tap into the elements more quickly next time."

"More quickly? Mom, are you serious? How can we all get into alignment and focus the elements much quicker than that?" Simone let out a sigh and headed back to the side of the house to plug the Edison bulbs back in.

"It's not a question for me." Jo led them back toward the house as she continued with Tavish trailing right behind her. "It's a connection you all must work on within yourselves, with your magic, and in connection with each other. As a coven, you must become one entity that breathes together, moves in tandem, and intuitively perceives what the whole intends to manifest. That is the beauty of a developed four-points coven."

Autumn bent down to grab Tavish from the ground and snuggle him into her sweater. "So, you're saying we're still working separately?"

Jo pushed the back door to the house open and turned to face Autumn behind her. "The trees don't think as they bend in the wind. They sense the air and react with innate knowing of what to do. A coven works in much the same way, and in time, you'll all move just like the trees in the wind."

CHAPTER 3

Autumn handed a kraft paper bag across the counter to a customer at Parchment and Pine and smiled softly. "Remember to tie your fortune to a tree branch to ensure the intention grows stronger."

The customer nodded with a big grin. "Yes, we'll remember. Thank you so much, Autumn!"

"You're so welcome! Enjoy the lunar new year!" Autumn waved as the customer walked out the front door of the shop, and she plopped down on a stool next to Simone behind the counter.

Simone turned to glare at her. "Do we ever have a slow season?"

"No, but that's actually a good thing. I am really grateful for how well the shop has done since we opened. I mean, even when we thought it was slow before the solstice, we ended up with tons of business. So as long as the steady stream of customers means we get to keep the doors open, then I'm happy and can't complain." Autumn fiddled with some twine behind the counter and pulled apart a few strands. "Who was on the phone a minute ago?"

"Oh, Mom called. She wants us over at the bath shop in a minute. I guess James brought his mother by there first, hoping my mom would give her some comfort. We better get over there and see what's going on." Simone turned off the computer screen and headed to the back for her coat.

"Sounds good. It's just about lunchtime, anyway, so it's a good time to close up for a while. Let me put some food out for Tavish, and then I'll be ready." Autumn made her way to the back and pulled out Tavish's bowls. He sauntered in with a big stretch of his paws and a yawn. "Aw, Tav. Were you curled up by the fire? It's lunchtime, cutie."

"Oh, I almost forgot." Simone wrapped her quilted coat around her and tucked her round Lennon sunglasses into her hair like a headband. "Mom said she called Chief Walsh to meet us at the shop as well. That way we all get the story at once."

Autumn nodded as she pulled her oatmeal-colored infinity scarf over her long auburn locks and threw on her light-gray wool coat. "Oh, okay. That's probably a good idea in case this turns out to be something serious. Plus . . . Ben might be with him."

Simone rolled her eyes as they walked to the front door. "Please. If Ben wants to see me, then he always knows where to find me. I'm not interested in playing games."

Autumn flipped the sign on the door to read "Will return in one hour" and pulled the door shut behind them. "Uh-huh. You can't fool me. I know you're just as smitten with him as he is with you. So don't pretend to not care if he comes around or not."

Walking down Main Street, the girls waved through the windows at their fellow shop owners. The hustle of the holiday season had recently ended, and the streets held a calming quiet to them. Yet, the posters were already going up for the coming Lunar Fair to mark the lunar new year in the mountain region. Although Hollow's Glenn wouldn't host the event, the entire region looked forward to fortune-telling, new year traditions, and the extra bit of sunlight that came right around that time.

The girls crossed and made their way to Jo's bath shop just as Chief Walsh and his son, Ben, arrived. The chief held the door open for them to enter.

"Autumn, Simone." The chief nodded and gave them a tight-lipped smile.

Once inside, the chief looked around to ensure no extra customers lingered around. He turned to flip the sign to "closed" so they could talk candidly.

"Oh, here they are now!" Jo opened her arms wide and welcomed everyone into the shop. "Please, everyone, come sit down over here." She directed them to a sofa and chairs on the far wall of the shop.

Penny sat beside Sorcha on the sofa and rubbed her forearm to comfort her as they greeted everyone. "Sorcha just returned from her sister's house. Apparently she's been missing for a few days now. Sorcha, dear, why don't you tell everyone what's happened?"

Sorcha looked up at Jo and James to get confirmation that she should begin. "Yes, I'm very worried, as I was supposed to meet Ayla at her home a few days ago. We usually get together every once in a while, and this time we planned to meet before the upcoming Lunar Fest. I knew she'd be heading to the festival as she does every year, so this was the perfect time to catch her beforehand. When I arrived, though, she was nowhere to be found."

"And you don't think she left early for the festival?" Jo gave Sorcha a sympathetic look.

"Oh, no. She wouldn't have gone before telling me first. Although, I did phone the festival chair, just in case, to see if he had seen her. He hadn't heard from her in several days either. I just know something's happened, and I can feel . . ." Sorcha paused, looking up at Chief Walsh and then at Jo again.

"It's all right, Sorcha. You can say anything in front of the chief and Ben. They know about our gifts and will keep it all confidential." Jo nodded reassuringly.

James sat down on the arm of the sofa beside his mother and grabbed her hand. "Mom, they're all here to help. So just tell us all the details you know."

"Yes, well, I felt that the energy was different in the house. A strange fogginess hung around the entire home, unlike anything I've experienced there before. I grew up in that house, and I'm very familiar with the energy. It's usually very uplifting and comforting, almost like the holidays year-round. But this time, it almost seemed cloudy." Sorcha squeezed her purse in her hands as she stared off into space.

Chief Walsh tilted his head down to meet Sorcha's eyes and bring her out of her daze. "Ma'am, has your sister ever disappeared like this before? Or wandered off without telling anyone?"

Sorcha shook her head as she thought. "Never. She does occasionally sleepwalk, but whenever that happens, she always stays near the home. Ayla's never gone far. And when her astral projection occurs, her body always stays where she fell asleep. So, in all these years, I've never known her to just disappear. I am concerned, though, that her husband may have come back and . . ." She choked up as she tried to get the words out. Holding back tears, she continued. "Well, let's just say that even with Ayla maintaining such a pleasant home, he wasn't the kindest to my sister throughout their marriage. It was all I could do for years to tell her to get rid of him. Finally, several months ago, she relented and separated from him, but now, I wonder if . . ."

"Sorcha, it's okay." Autumn crossed her legs in her chair and leaned in closer toward Ayla. "We'll take things one step at a time and look into every possibility. Did you look around the entire property for her while you were there?"

"It's such a large place that I only searched around the perimeter of the house. Although, I'm sure I would have sensed her nearby if she were anywhere on the property. We have a strong connection between us, and when we're far apart, we each feel an emptiness. I'm not sure how to explain it, but I sense that she's gone. I'm so fearful because I can't connect with her energy at all."

Autumn sighed and looked up at the chief. "If it's okay with you, I'd like to go look around the property. On the letter where Sorcha described the disappearance, there was a strange lunar eclipse stamp that glistened with magic. Sorcha, do you know anything about the magic on that paper?"

Sorcha shook her head as she remembered the stationery. "I'm afraid not. I did notice the shimmers, but I don't know where that stationery came from. I just assumed Ayla made it herself and left it on the desk. I've never seen it before, though."

"There may be more to this than meets the eye," Autumn suggested. "And if you send your deputies out, they may miss something important." She gave Ian Walsh a serious look, implying that she was ready to take on whatever lay ahead.

Sorcha interjected with appreciation. "Autumn, thank you! I'd feel so much better knowing our four-points witch was looking into Ayla's disappearance. I trust you to find her and bring her back safely!"

The chief looked at Autumn and then around the room for a moment. "Autumn, I've seen you do some pretty incredible things these past few months. So, if you tell me there may be something beyond the norm going on here, then I'm inclined to believe you and give you a head start on this. I'll have my officers get a statement from Sorcha later this afternoon and log the missing person, but we'll have to work with the town where Ayla lives on this one. I can buy you some time to go over there and see what you can find, though. But . . ."—the chief raised his forefinger and eyed Autumn—"I want James to go with you, and you're not to disturb anything you find. If there is something more magical going on here, then we're gonna have a hard enough time as it is to solidify the case. So, do me a favor and keep any evidence you find intact." The chief looked over at James to get his understanding.

James nodded. "I understand, Chief. I'll stay with Autumn, and we'll be sure to keep everything the way we find it."

"I'll have my radio on me at all times today, and so will Ben." The chief turned to his son to confirm his agreement with a head nod. "If you run into any trouble, call the station immediately. They'll dispatch some local officers, and I'll be right behind them. But please, don't make me regret waiting."

Autumn stood from her chair and shook her head. "Not for a second, Chief." She slid her hands firmly into her coat pockets and met eyes with everyone around the room, stopping at James. "Let's go see the unseen."

CHAPTER 4

James pulled out the keys his mother had given him for Ayla's home. He inserted one into the lock and carefully pushed the front door open with Autumn close behind him. An eerie stillness lingered in the house, and Autumn immediately picked up the smell of herbs in the air.

"Hmm, I smell thyme." Autumn put her hand on James's back. "Do you smell it, too, or is it just me?"

Shaking his head, he looked back at her. "No, it's just you. I can't smell anything, but it does feel stuffy in here. I guess my mother didn't bother to open any windows, and no one else has been around in quite some time, it seems." James walked through each adjoining room in the house, starting in the front entryway by the stairs and working his way through the living room, dining room, and kitchen at the back. "No sign of anyone. I'm going to check upstairs."

"Okay, sounds good." Autumn lingered in the living room, carefully searching for any clues. A warmth came over her chest, and she put her hand on the locket she wore from her late grandmother. She knew the magical green glow of it electrified underneath her sweater.

As the locket's heat pulsated under her palm, it signaled to Autumn that she stood close to something important. She stopped at a small roll-top desk with papers strewn on top. Lying in plain sight sat the ink-stamped linen papers that Sorcha had used days earlier. "I found the eclipse paper," Autumn called to James. "There are a few here, but…" Autumn looked up as James stomped down the stairs. She pulled her gloves out of her pockets and put them on before lifting one of the papers up into the light. "The ink is still wet."

James walked over and eyed the paper curiously. "How can that be if Ayla's been gone for several days?"

A chill crept up Autumn's spine. "Unless someone else has been here."

"No one else was with my mother when she was here, and she found these papers lying around to use for her letter. So if these are still wet, then someone made a few of the stamped papers before my mother arrived and a few after she left." James looked around the house one more time. "I don't like this. Let's go outside."

Autumn nodded and headed out the front door alongside James. "We need to search the entire property before we go. She may be out there hurt or something."

He agreed hesitantly. "You're right, but stay close to me, okay?"

"Yeah, okay. Let's start out back. It looks like the property goes out quite a ways." Autumn followed the wraparound porch to the back side of the house and moved down the steps to a hard clay ground slippery with loose gravel and rocks. "I didn't expect it to be so rocky out here."

James walked ahead a few steps and turned his head to reply. "Yeah, that's typical for this area. The property is fairly large, but I'm mostly concerned with this close section near the tree line and the river. If we head straight back, we'll hit the water's edge where the river meets the rock. These nice trees on the side of the house line the edge of the property all the way to the river, but otherwise, it's mostly rock out here for a few acres beyond that."

Autumn stepped carefully across the gravel terrain as they made their way closer toward the tree line. "It's actually really beautiful in a stark way. And I can already hear the water."

"It's just down here a few more steps. The end of these trees marks the waterline." James lifted his hand out to the left of them as they followed the line of pine trees.

Autumn moved closer to the tree line and scanned the ground for any traces of Ayla. It felt dry beneath her feet, and the air sat completely still around her. She squinted at the trees and noticed one standing out in the foreground of an otherwise pine forest. She recognized it as a hawthorn tree, similar to the one that stood in the forest between the girls' cottage and Mrs. Pendleton's home. The tree represented the namesake of the home passed down from their grandmother, Hawthorn Cottage, and she recalled the peculiar magic always surrounding it.

"Autumn, over here!" James called, shaking her out of her memory.

"Okay, I'm coming!" Autumn quickly ran over to him as he knelt on the rocky ground, observing marks in the gravel. "What is it?"

"Looks like something got dragged along here. The marks go back toward the house, so we must have missed them while we were walking closer to the trees." James stood up and turned toward the house and then back the other way toward the river. "Let's see where they lead." He continued moving toward the water as Autumn stayed close behind.

They both scanned the horizon as the gravel crunched under their boots and the drag marks stretched out in front of them. Once they reached the water's edge, the marks faded into the sandy tide. James looked up and down the edge before setting his eyes on something toward the tree line.

"James, I smell the thyme in the air again. Be careful!" Autumn tried to keep up with him as his pace increased.

He stopped at a rocky outcropping and climbed up onto the ledge under the tree line. "Autumn, you better call the station."

Catching up to him at the rocky ledge, she peered up at him while trying to slow her breath. "Is it Ayla?"

James looked down at the lifeless body folded over on the ground and shook his head. "No, it's not her... So the question is, whose dead body am I standing over?"

As the medics strapped the body to a stretcher, James and Autumn watched from the river's edge. Autumn held James's arm tightly with her own and focused her attention on the officers combing the property. She squinted as one bent down and picked something up at the water's edge.

"What does he have?" Autumn leaned into James and asked.

James directed his attention to two police officers standing in the water as waves pushed over their boots on the rocky shore. He took a couple steps closer to them with Autumn right beside him. "Looks like a cell phone. Maybe this guy dropped it before his murder." James lifted his chin toward the body being hauled away on the stretcher.

Autumn casually took a few steps toward the officers and tried to glance down at the phone in one's hand. "Uh, excuse me. I don't mean to interrupt, but I was wondering what more you needed from us. Someone got our statements a minute ago." Autumn quickly glanced down to see a picture on the screen of the phone.

A familiar voice came from behind her and interjected. "It's all right, Officer. I can finish up with this witness. You go ahead with collecting evidence."

Relieved to hear Chief Walsh, Autumn turned and found him standing beside James and Ben. "Chief, I'm glad you're here."

"Autumn." The chief gave her a worried look. "When I gave you that head start, I was hoping to keep things under the radar."

She curled her lip up to one side as if feeling the sting of what just happened. "Yeah, I know. I seem to always be in the middle of something. But apparently that's where I'm meant to be these days."

The chief nodded and looked between Autumn and James. "So I've heard." He sighed. "Well, the Blake County Sheriff's Department has jurisdiction over this now since the death happened in their area. I'm gonna try to keep a foot in the investigation since Ayla's missing person's report got filed with us in Hollow's Glenn, but it may be hard to keep tabs on this one."

"We understand, Chief, and we appreciate anything you can do to help us bring Ayla home safely." Autumn grabbed James's hand and gave him a tight-lipped smile.

"Autumn's right. My family trusts you, Chief." James gave the chief and Ben a serious look. "We need your help on this one to get my aunt back."

The chief thought for a moment while eyeing James. He cleared his throat and relented with a sympathetic look. "Well, I know I'll never hear the end of it from Jo if I let this one go. And I don't believe my conscience will let me get over it either."

"What do you wanna do, Chief?" Ben stared at his father, waiting for their next move.

"I already know the gist of what's going on here, so why don't you start by telling me what you just saw that officer pick up on the shore here?" Chief Walsh rested his hands on his belt and gave Autumn a chance to gather her thoughts.

She took a few steps forward on the wet rocks and recalled what the officer was holding a few moments ago. "I came over here because I noticed the other officer picking something up in the water. When I came to talk to him, I realized it was a cell phone with the screen cracked slightly. A photo of a woman took up the screen. From what I could quickly see, she was standing right here by the water's edge, and . . ." Autumn paused, looking out into the water to make sense of what she had seen.

Ben stepped up beside her. "Go ahead, Autumn. You can tell us the whole story."

She held her hands up in front of her, one slightly closer than the other. "There appeared to be another silhouette behind her reflected in the water . . . but a dark flare of some sort blurred it out."

"A dark flare and a second reflection," the chief repeated. "That's interesting. I'll check with the sheriff's office about it, but I'm guessing you think there's more to it than just the camera lens flaring."

Autumn nodded. "Yeah, something doesn't seem right to me. There's more to it, but I can't pinpoint what, exactly."

"Well, I'll follow up with the local department on it, Chief," Ben interjected. "If Autumn thinks it's something, then it probably is."

"Good. What else can you both tell me that I won't find out from the officers on the ground?"

"Well, they know we walked the property and then found drag marks running toward the river. But I didn't tell anyone besides James that . . ."—Autumn turned and faced Ayla's house across the rocky land—"I got a strange smell of thyme inside Ayla's home, along with finding wet ink stamps just like the one on the letter Sorcha wrote a few days ago."

"Wet ink, huh?" The chief looked at her curiously when a scream came from out in the distance.

"No, Philip! Not my Philip!" A woman's voice carried across the land.

Chief Walsh gave his son a nod, and Ben ran through the property to get closer to the woman. Autumn, James, and Chief Walsh followed behind as quickly as they could.

"Please, just give me another minute with him before you take him away," the distraught woman yelled at the medics.

"I'm sorry, ma'am, but you'll have to come down to the coroner's office to confirm his identity officially." A medic covered the man's face back up with the sheet and continued wheeling him toward the ambulance at the front of the property.

The woman dropped to the ground and covered her face in her hands. Ben bent down beside her and put his hand on her shoulder.

"I know this is hard, ma'am, but can you tell me who you are?" Ben softened his tone as he spoke to the woman.

Pulling her head out of her hands, she watched as the medics loaded the man into the ambulance. "He was only out here to make sure she was all right. She was all alone these days."

Ben looked up to find his father standing with James and Autumn. He sighed and shifted to help the woman up off the ground. "What's your name, ma'am? Let's start with that."

"Amelia. Amelia Gibson." She fought back more tears as she tried to get the words out. "And that's my husband, Philip. My poor Philip."

"All right, Mrs. Gibson, can you tell me if you live around here?" Ben held her steady so she wouldn't collapse to the ground beside him.

The woman raised her arm and pointed in the distance. "Yes, over there. My house sits across the street, and I saw all the commotion. I've been waiting on my Philip to return." She sobbed and doubled over. "I knew for years that this family was trouble, but I let him come over here in the middle of the night because we thought Ayla was all alone. Those darn peculiar lights were sparking up like crazy, making our dog start a howl. Well, after that I couldn't find him since, and no one's been home here." A bitter look drew across her face. "Now my poor Philip is gone because of them."

"Okay, ma'am, so you both saw lights. And, Mrs. Gibson, what did you mean when you said he's gone because of them?" Chief Walsh leaned in and attempted to put a comforting hand on her back as she cried.

"Because of their arguments and problems, and then . . ."—she looked up at the moon in the evening sky with anger—"because of that moon."

Jo's New Moon Intentions Bath

When the moon is dark or shows a sliver of a waxing crescent, run a cooling bath. Add the following ingredients to the tub:

1 Tbsp epsom salt

1 Tbsp black salt

2 Tbsp lavender flowers

3-5 drops lavender essential oil

Place a few purple crystals around the outer edge of the tub. Step into the cool water as you consider your intentions for this new moon cycle. Using your hands, let the water gently wash over your face and scalp. Chant the following words three times:

My clear intentions manifest in my reality.

Submerge your body in the bath and allow yourself to float within the water for a few moments as you consider your intentions. When you're ready, drain the bath water fully before stepping out of the tub and drying off.

CHAPTER 5

Autumn pushed the front door open to her gran's cottage, and James followed behind her inside. Simone sat on the living room sofa, removing her running shoes while Tavish took a bath beside her.

"Where have you guys been? I expected you hours ago, but Aunt Penny helped me close up the shop for the day." Simone threw her shoes on the floor and flopped back on the couch with a sigh. "I just got back from my long run tonight. I think I'm getting my groove back after finding Mr. Leslie on my riverside run."

Autumn dropped her backpack and coat at the door and made her way into the living room. "Well, that's one good thing, I guess. Today was not the best day." Autumn raised her eyebrows at her cousin.

James concurred. "Yeah, we've been at my aunt Ayla's property this whole time."

Simone sat up abruptly. "You found her?"

Autumn shook her head. "No, but we found the neighbor doubled over on a cliff ledge next to the river. His wife saw the commotion and wandered over from across the street and identified him. She mentioned that he'd gone over there during the eclipse, but she hadn't seen him since and had been worried sick about where he might have gone. I guess she never thought the worst."

"Whoa, okay. So, a dead body showed up, but it's not Ayla, thankfully. Was there any sign of her? Or what happened to this other guy?" Simone crossed her legs underneath her and straightened up to listen more intently.

"We don't really know anything more at this point," James chimed in, sitting on the arm of the couch and petting Tavish. "We found some strange clues, like a wet ink stamp on some papers, same as the stamp at the top of my mom's letter. Then, there was the smell of thyme in the house."

"Thyme? What does that herb mean?" Simone scrunched up her nose while she thought.

"I'm not really sure. All I could think of was how Gran used to wrap thyme bundles together and place them on the porches of first responders. I think they were supposed to be for courage and strength."

"Well, that sounds intense. Maybe we should ask our moms about that one. Or Eve might know, too. She's getting really good with her earth magic, using different herbs and spices."

"You're right. I bet Eve would know what it is. Plus, I wanna start relying on our coven rather than our mothers for all the answers. We've gotta stand on our own at some point, right?" Autumn opened her arms to welcome Tavish onto her lap and give him a petting.

"Don't forget to tell Simone about the cell phone they found at the scene, too." James stood up and headed toward the door.

"Cell phone, huh?" Simone glanced up at him curiously.

"Oh, and Chief Walsh and his son came to the scene to support the local investigation." James pointed his thumb toward the door. "I've gotta get back and check on my parents tonight. They'll want an update about today, and I wanna be the one to give it to them before they hear rumors around town."

Autumn scooped Tavish into her arms and met James at the door. "Thanks for going out there with me today. I'm sorry we don't know what happened to your aunt, but there's still hope we'll find her safe."

James brushed the long locks away from Autumn's face and kissed her lips. "I'm hopeful if you are. Keep me updated if you find anything else, and I'll talk to you soon. Bye, Simone." James waved from the doorway and headed out.

Autumn moved toward the kitchen at the back of the house. "I'm starving. Have you eaten anything yet?"

"No, I wanted to get my run in first. We've got some broccoli and cheese hand pies that are just waiting to be thrown into the oven. Wanna toss those in while I take a quick shower? And then you can tell me more about this cell phone and everything else you found out there." Simone lifted her eyebrows up and down a couple times in suggestion when a knock came at the front door.

Placing Tavish down on the ground, Autumn moved around the kitchen island toward the front entry. "James must have forgotten something. I'll get it." Autumn pulled the cottage door open to find an unexpected visitor standing in front of her. Taken aback, Autumn's mouth dropped open. "Anabeth . . ."

The local newspaper reporter who had angered Mrs. Leslie a few months back after printing a story about her dead husband now stood at their doorstep. She had redeemed herself through helping save a couple lives, including Autumn's, so that counted for a lot. And now, she knew the MacKinnon secrets and that of the town as well.

"Hey, Autumn. I'm sorry to bother you at home, but . . . can I come in?" She pressed her teeth together and waited for a response.

"Okay, yeah. Simone and I were just about to make some hand pies for dinner. Would you like to join us?" Autumn let Anabeth in and turned to see Simone shaking her head no in the background. She tilted her head and gave her cousin a smirk.

"Uh, I don't want to cause any extra work." Anabeth followed Autumn to the kitchen and removed her coat, throwing it over a kitchen stool.

Waving her hand in the air, Autumn began removing the hand pies from a container in the fridge and neatly preparing them for the oven. "It's no trouble. I already prepped the pastries and filled them all the other night. So, I'm just gonna put a couple of these into the oven. One more will fill the tray nicely."

Simone grabbed three glasses from the cabinet and filled them all with water. "So, what's going on, Anabeth?" She handed a glass across the island to their visitor.

"Well, Autumn, I was in Blake County earlier today, doing some research into this illegal fracking that's been going on all over the region, when our police scanners went off and directed us over to the old Ross property on the river, and . . ." Anabeth took a sip of her water and cleared her throat. "My photographer snapped a photo of you and James leaving the scene. You appeared to be standing near the body being taken away."

Simone sighed. "Anabeth, are you seriously here trying to get the first scoop on this story?"

Anabeth threw her hands up and shook her head. "No, really, I'm not. I just wanted to let you know it will be coming out. I'm sorry they got a picture of you, Autumn, but I'm pretty sure they're gonna run it."

Autumn threw the sheet pan into the oven and let her shoulders dip down. "It's okay, Anabeth. We were there, so there's no use covering any of it up."

"So . . . completely off the record, but is there something magical going on here?" Anabeth peered at them both over the rim of her water glass before taking a sip.

"Honestly, we have no idea." Autumn came around to sit on one of the other kitchen stools. "Ayla Ross is missing, so something strange is definitely going on. Whether or not it's magical has yet to be determined. All I know is that her sister, Sorcha, trusts us to uncover what happened and to find her, even more than she trusts the police. That's why we were out there."

"Well, please let me know if I can help. Honestly, I really do wanna help. If I hear something unusual about the case, I'll let you know. I mean, there have been a lot of crazy things going on in our mountain region lately. Every time I turn around it's something about mysterious lights in the mountains or stealing of resources from the lands. There's a new story running about these things at least a couple times a week." She paused and thought for a moment, trying to piece things together. "Is this all part of this magical underground I'm just learning about?"

Autumn and Simone exchanged glances and laughed. Simone nodded through her big grin. "Magical underground, huh? I like the sound of that. It makes us seem so stealthy and shadowy."

Anabeth rolled her eyes. "I don't know what to call it, just that it's all new to me and that I'm fascinated by your gifts. I wish I could bend water to my will and make birds send messages to whomever I chose."

Autumn propped her head up on her arm. "Anabeth, I know it sounds cool to have these gifts, but sometimes they're really more of a burden. My life has changed so much recently now that I'm the four-points witch and expected to bring all the elements together again and lead the founding families. I've taken on the responsibility because it's important to our community and our lands, but it's taking a toll on me. I don't know about Simone, but I miss normal everyday life."

Simone shook her head. "Yeah, I mean, I love being part of a coven with you and getting to solve these interesting mysteries. But you're right. Normal everyday life was awesome, even though we always had a little magic in our days."

"Well, I'm sorry this is a lot of responsibility on you both. But I'm confident that if people really knew all that you did for the mountain region, they'd be extremely grateful. Seriously, you're like underground magical superheroes who are normal business owners by day. I kind of love that about both of you, and I also love that I get to be part of it now, too. So, please let me know how I can keep helping, okay?"

Autumn smiled at her and nodded. "Okay. Now, let's grab those hand pies and start eating. The smell of that bubbling cheese is calling my name."

"Yes, please! Oh, and one more thing before I forget. When I was interviewing the other families on the street near the Ross property, several of them confirmed seeing those strange mountain lights nearby . . . specifically on the night of the lunar eclipse."

Autumn exchanged a serious look with Simone and thought out loud. "The same night Ayla possibly went missing."

CHAPTER 6

"**S**im! Where are you?" Autumn rushed around the house the next morning, throwing her gray wool coat on and scooping up Tavish into a flannel-lined basket. "Where is she, Tav? We have to open the shop!"

Autumn grabbed her brown faux-suede backpack in her other hand and did her best to pull the front door open with full hands. Peering out into the yard, she spotted Simone with her camera. "I was looking for you everywhere. We've gotta go!"

"I'm ready! I just wanted to snap some nature photos for our new patterns before we head to the shop. I really love the shapes of the tree branches this time of year, and I wanna capture that before the leaves sprout again." Simone knelt on the grass and pointed her camera lens toward the trees between Hawthorn Cottage and the Pendletons' home next door. "Just let me get one more shot . . . Got it! Okay, I'm ready."

Simone got up from the ground and started putting her camera gear back into her vegan leather bag while Autumn headed to the SUV with Tavish. Just as they both put their heads down, a flash of light sparked in the trees.

Simone looked up instantly. "Did you see that?"

Autumn softly stepped away from the SUV and nodded. "I think so. A flash of light?"

"Yeah, it was almost like a camera flash. I think it came from the trees out here by Mrs. Pendleton's house." Simone took a few steps closer to the woods. "Weird. It's almost got the same purple energy I've felt looming in the mountains, but now that I'm focused on these trees, it feels a lot lighter right here."

Darting her eyes around the grounds to find some other clues, Autumn hesitated when she glimpsed a hint of a bluish shimmer on the forest floor. She walked closer to the tree line as a few more sapphire-blue lights glinted around, dotting the base of the trees before fading.

"The wisps," Autumn whispered under her breath.

The trees swayed as the wind picked up and sent her hair swirling around her. She sensed the voices of her ancestors who occasionally spoke to her arise again.

"The doorways are open. Prepare for the light and the dark." The whispers lingered in Autumn's ears as her focus remained on the forest.

"Autumn, what is it? Did you see something?" Simone put one hand on Autumn's shoulder and snapped her fingers in front of Autumn's face with the other.

Shaking out of her daze, Autumn regained awareness of Simone beside her. "Sorry, yeah. I saw . . . something I had seen long ago. And the voices came back."

"Oh! We're back to hearing voices again? Okay." Simone put her arm around her cousin and walked her back to the SUV. "What did they have to say this time?"

Autumn hopped into the car as Tavish jumped onto her lap from the back seat. "They mentioned a doorway being opened, and . . ."—Autumn swallowed hard, taking comfort in Tavish's eyes—"being ready for light and dark."

"Okay . . . Well, we could look at that as a glass half empty or half full. What do you think?" Simone started the car and turned to Autumn for a response.

"At the rate we're going, I'm afraid to say." Autumn pressed the radio on and switched it to a slow Fleetwood Mac song. She leaned back and closed her eyes as Tavish jumped behind her seat. "Let's just see where the day takes us. Something tells me Eve will be the first one through our door today, and it won't be just to deliver pastries."

Simone started the fire in the hearth room as Autumn lit a few pine-scented candles around their Parchment and Pine paper shop. The front door chimed, and Tavish trotted up to be the first one to greet their visitor.

Eve took a step inside and bent down to give the cat a rub. "Hi, Tavish. You're looking awfully cute today." She stood up and walked toward the back counter with her arms loaded with a large Forest Brew bag. "Hey, it's just me. I'm bringing over some fresh pastries and baked goods for you to sell. I've got lots of winter spice and powdered sugar donuts. I don't know why, but I keep thinking about donuts lately. They've been on my mind so much! Plus, I brought mini apple turnovers, orange-glazed pound cake, and some lavender vanilla madeleine cookies."

Autumn turned her head in Simone's direction and smirked before heading back to join Eve at the checkout counter. "Eve, you're right on time, and everything smells amazing! I don't know if I can resist snacking on a couple things before we put it all out to sell. We should taste test it first, right?"

Eve laughed and bunched up her hands at her mouth to cover her smile. "I'm just so happy that the pastries have been a success! Thank you both so much for offering to sell some here to your customers! We've been getting new orders left and right at the Forest Brew, and my parents are thrilled."

"Then let's keep this pastry train running! But, of course, I'm heading for a donut first." Simone walked up and opened the Forest Brew bag as the warm scent of baked goods wafted out. "Wow, good thing my leggings are stretchy. I'll grab a platter from the back."

"So, this isn't all you came over for this morning, am I right?" Autumn removed the goodies from the bag as Simone returned with the platter for a display.

Eve slid onto a counter stool and watched the girls display her beautiful baked goods and pastries as she nervously spoke. "Actually, no. There's been a lot of chatter in the coffee shop this morning. A brand new stack of newspapers got delivered, and right on the front page sat a big picture of Autumn and James."

Autumn sighed. "Yeah, Anabeth came by last night to tell us about that one. It's okay, Eve. I'm not worried about it."

"You're not? That's a relief. So . . . have you also heard that Ayla's ex-husband is back in town?" Eve poked her finger out to move a couple madeleine cookies around on the tray and show off their luscious vanilla lavender drizzle.

"What? Ex-husband?" Autumn stopped what she was doing behind the counter to listen more intently to Eve.

"Yeah, I heard a few customers talking about seeing him in town after he was gone for a while. I think his name's Brodie Aitken. Anyway, it sounds like he's lurking around and trying to move back into Ayla's house." Eve swiveled her stool left and right a bit as she spoke.

"Are they divorced or just separated?" Simone moved behind the computer and started it up for the day. She brought up a few calendar designs as she thought. "I thought they just split, and he'd been gone for a while."

Autumn lifted a pen in the air and shook it between her fingers. "Actually, I don't know if they ever divorced. Sorcha said the Ross family was never fond of him, though. It sounded like she had tried for years to get her sister to leave him, but Ayla only recently kicked him out. That doesn't mean they got a divorce, though, so who knows what he's up to."

"Huh, so do you think he's back because he heard she went missing, or do you think he may be behind her disappearance?" Eve spun completely around in a circle on her stool and stopped herself with her hands on the counter.

Simone peeked out from behind the computer and twisted her mouth around at Eve. "You're making me dizzy. Can you stop fidgeting while we talk?"

Autumn smiled to herself at Simone's comment and put her head down to cut some ribbon behind the counter.

"Sorry, I get antsy and have to do something with my energy. But, as far as this ex-husband goes, if the Ross family never liked him, then maybe he's a bit of an unsavory character we should look into." Eve squinted her eyes and nodded at the girls.

"I agree." Autumn tied a quick bow around a large paper calendar and set it aside. "Who would show up out of the blue after their ex goes missing? That sounds very suspicious and worthy of questioning. I'm just not sure how we'll question him about it, but we'll add him to the suspect list." Autumn walked the calendar over to a round table in the center of the shop and stood it up against a wooden crate filled with other new calendars.

"So, that's suspect number one, then?" Simone stood up and made her way to the front window of the shop to look out at all the quaint boutiques on Main Street. The traffic started picking up for the day, and she could feel the deep purple aura looming over the distant mountains.

"Yep, that's number one." Autumn clipped a few red paper fortunes to a long hanging piece of twine with clothespins near the front window. "And I think I know where we might get a tip on suspect number two. Simone, let's take a long lunch break today and find out."

"Okay . . . Where are we headed?" Simone slid her hands into the back pockets of her stretchy black jean leggings and gave Autumn a questioning look.

"To have a little chat with the chair of the Lunar Fair." Autumn looked up to the ceiling at a moon phase pendant hanging down. She blew a powerful breath out toward the paper pendant and made it spin swiftly in circles. "Sorcha mentioned Ayla wasn't there to set up her booth for next weekend, but I bet whoever's running the event still has some information they can share."

CHAPTER 7

Autumn cranked up the heat as Simone drove the two of them up a winding mountain road toward Blake County. Simone glared at her cousin and shook her head.

"You're smoking us out here! Would you stop turning the heat so high?" Simone sighed and tugged at the collar of her black chunky knit sweater.

Autumn rubbed her hands over her chilly arms. "Sorry, I just can't seem to get warm with this cold snap we're getting today. But I guess February is usually our coldest month, and it's just about here. I bet they're going to need lots of heaters outside for the Lunar Fair this time."

"Yeah, and maybe a big bonfire, too, at this rate. I thought the cold might wrap up early this year, but maybe not. Heck, now I'm guessing we'll have snow until May!" Simone turned her SUV down a dirt path marked with a big sign that read County Fairgrounds.

"Good, we're here. Just pull in down there." Autumn pointed ahead toward a large building that looked like a main office.

Simone nodded and parked beside a big black pickup truck in a lot with a few sporadic cars. "Looks like someone's here. Ready?"

Autumn wrapped her infinity scarf around her neck once more and grabbed her backpack off the floor. "Yep, let's go."

The two of them headed for the front door of the building as the dark-green flag of the mountain region swung back and forth, clanking against a tall flagpole.

"The wind is picking up out here. Is that you?" Simone squinted at her cousin.

"No, I'm not doing anything. There's just an eeriness to this area that I can't put my finger on." Autumn looked around them and felt as though eyes were watching from afar.

"You're right. I feel it, too. It didn't seem like this last year when we came out here for the Lunar Fest, but something's changed." Simone pulled the heavy glass door open for Autumn.

"Thanks. Let's just do what we came here to do and get back to Hollow's Glenn." Autumn led the way through the entry toward a large circular desk with an older woman barely visible behind it other than the gray bun atop her head. With a smile,

Autumn got the woman's attention. "Hello, we're looking for the Lunar Fest chairperson."

"That's Jake Doyle." The woman looked over the edge of her glasses at Autumn. "He oversees all the major events here at the fairgrounds. I'll fetch him for you." She put a phone to her ear and dialed a few numbers. "Mr. Doyle, a couple ladies are here to see you." She hung up the phone and gave Autumn a smile. "He'll be out in just a moment. Go ahead and have a seat."

Simone waved at her. "Thanks."

As the girls sat down, a shout came from the back office. "I need that slot filled ASAP! We can't have any open booths for the new year or we won't meet our vendor quotas. And with the publicity for this event, you and I both need to make sure we look good." A clean-shaven man in a full suit stormed toward the front desk at them in a huff. As he raised his arm to smooth his hair while he walked briskly, Autumn noticed a silver four-leaf-clover cufflink on his sleeve. The man appeared to have money and power behind him, and he wasn't afraid to use it. He blew past the girls, through the front doors, and straight to his car.

Simone raised her eyebrows at Autumn. "Man, someone is not happy."

Another man walked out from the back and approached them. "Ladies, sorry about the wait. I'm the festival chair. What can I do for you?"

Autumn stood up and put her right hand out to shake his. "Hello, Mr. Doyle. I'm Autumn MacKinnon, and this is my cousin, Simone. We're actually here about Ayla Ross Aitken, who has a festival booth. The family hasn't seen her in a few days, and we wondered if she'd come by at all."

Mr. Doyle sighed. "Oh yes, Ayla Ross. I believe she started using her maiden name just recently. Yes, she's done the festival for years now, and we all really loved having her tarot reading as part of our event. But unfortunately, since I haven't heard from her, I'm going to have to let that booth go to someone else."

"Oh, I see." Autumn thought for a moment. "She hasn't come by to confirm the booth, put a down payment down, or anything at all?" Autumn didn't believe Ayla could have been so absent with the new year just a few days away.

Mr. Doyle walked over to the front desk and signed a few papers that the woman laid out for him. "Well, yes, she has already done quite a bit to secure her booth for this year. Typically, Ayla comes to all our planning meetings ahead of the fair. She already attended a few and helped with some marketing efforts, but then she just vanished. I haven't seen her for about a week now, and we can't afford to just let things drop off. I have to answer to all the higher-ups who want everything to run smoothly, you know."

"That sounds strange that she would just vanish like that and not come back to help with something she was so invested in. Did anything unusual happen that you know of?" Simone chimed in and moved closer to the desk, resting her elbow on it casually to encourage the conversation with more ease.

Mr. Doyle's mouth dropped open as if ready to say something, but then he paused. "Who did you say you both were again?"

Autumn put her hand over her heart and spoke softly. "Oh, we're close with the Ross family. We're all concerned about Ayla's well-being since she's gone missing."

"Missing, you say?" Mr. Doyle interjected, and the woman behind the counter rose, covering her hand over her mouth. Seeing her distraught, he put his arm on her shoulder for comfort.

Autumn gave them both a solemn look. "Yes, has no one told you?"

"Well, her sister called the other day, asking if we'd seen Ayla around, but I told her none of us had." The woman wrapped her handknit cardigan around her waist. "I didn't realize she'd gone missing. That's awful!"

"What can we do?" Mr. Doyle questioned. "We're all devastated that she isn't around to brighten up the place this year, and it's terrible to think something's really happened to her. Mrs. Birch, take down their information so we can help." He directed the woman behind the desk, pointing to a paper and pen.

Simone took the paper from Mrs. Birch and wrote the contact information for Parchment and Pine while Autumn continued.

"Well, any information you can give us would be helpful. Was there anyone who might have been upset with Ayla or . . ."—Autumn hesitated—"wanted her out of the picture for any reason?"

Sighing, Mr. Doyle rubbed his forehead with his hand. "My goodness, there seems to be quite a bit of trouble this year. Let's see . . . For starters, the last time Ayla came, a man burst into our meeting and got very upset at her. It was something about a tarot reading she had done for his mother. Sounded like it cost him his inheritance, and he was very adamant that he wasn't going to just let it blow over."

"Geez! That's definitely something to look into!" Simone handed the contact information to Mrs. Birch and propped her chin up with her arm to continue listening.

Mrs. Birch pulled out some knitting needles hooked through a small scarf from underneath the desk and began clicking them together. "Go on, Jake. Tell them what else."

Autumn perked up. "Something else happened?"

"Oh, it's just that Ayla's booth ranks as highly coveted around here. She's our star fortune teller for the new year event and has been for years. She gets prime positioning for her booth and lots of airtime on all the news channels. Plus, this year we have a lot of publicity riding on the festival, and a major publisher coming down from the city. They wanted to potentially sign Ayla for a book deal, but now that she's gone . . ." He met eyes with Mrs. Birch, who glanced up from her knitting with pursed lips.

"People have pestered us left and right for days now over that booth." Mrs. Birch shook her head as she clicked away with her knitting needles.

"Pestered? Like other people want the booth and her publicity?" Simone leaned toward Mrs. Birch and nodded as if they were on the same wavelength.

Mr. Doyle threw his hands up. "The thing is, I'm getting so much pressure to make this event a success. We need to keep all the booth spaces filled, and the fortune-telling booth is the most important of all for the lunar new year. So I've got the county commissioners breathing down my neck, and now . . ." Rubbing his face again with both hands, he looked up at the girls with worry. "I've got one very aggressive palm reader who just won't let go of the fact that she deserves to have that booth. It's all I can do to not let it go to her. She's unrelenting." He shook his head vigorously.

"I honestly don't even know why she thinks it's available. Who's told her Ayla is gone?" Mrs. Birch knitted even more furiously now.

"Wait, so this palm reader has been calling relentlessly, hoping to take that booth, and no one advertised that it's available?" Autumn propped her hands on her hips and thought about it. "Sounds suspiciously opportunistic. Do you know where we could find this palm reader, by any chance?"

A couple men dressed in overalls and work jackets burst through the entry door and stomped their boots on the mat.

Mr. Doyle turned his back on the men and moved closer to Autumn so as not to be heard.

"Delia Hall is the woman you're looking for. I believe she's from Hollow's Glenn, but I know she frequents the apothecary in Ivansedge. If you go looking for her, keep your head about you. There's something not right about Delia or that apothecary." Mr. Doyle turned abruptly and patted Autumn on the back, raising his voice. "Well, thanks for stopping in! We can't wait to see you at the Lunar Fest this coming weekend!"

The two workers made their way toward the desk and eyed Autumn and Simone curiously. They handed Mrs. Birch a few pages of what looked to be yellow inventory slips and wiped their dirty hands on some rags she pulled out from behind the counter.

Autumn got the message that it was time to go and made her way to the door with Simone close behind. "Thank you! See you at the festival!"

The girls made their way out to Simone's SUV and hopped in quickly, driving away through the dirt parking lot now filled with forklifts and delivery vans. Autumn glanced around to see materials coming into the fairgrounds.

"Well, you were right," Simone noted as she switched the radio to classic rock and drove onto the curvy mountain road. "We got a second suspect out of this."

Autumn looked out the side window as she thought. "Yeah, and a third. That angry man with the outburst at their meeting. It sounded like he'd had an axe to grind with Ayla for pushing him out of his inheritance. The question is, who was that man?"

"Could have been anyone related to Ayla's client," Simone suggested.

"Exactly, so we'll have to find out who Ayla's client was first and then determine the upset heir in question. But since that one's unclear right now, we better make a stop in Ivansedge." Autumn pulled a tiny silver tube of calendula lotion out of her backpack and rubbed it onto her dry hands. "You like mysterious apothecaries, don't you?"

CHAPTER 8

An antique black sign hung above the door with ivory script letters, reading Rhiannon Apothecary. It creaked as it swung back and forth in the now howling wind.

Autumn pushed the shop door open and slowly walked inside as Simone followed. Rows of tall apothecary shelves lined the side walls, and glass terrariums with interesting vines draped down from the ceiling.

"Come in," a voice echoed from the back as long bead strands clattered in the archway. A middle-aged woman emerged with dark, slightly graying tight spiral curls springing out from her head past her shoulders. Long black tourmaline crystals hung down from her ears, and her dark skin glowed luminously under the warm light of abundant candles.

Simone read her aura as a layered light purple and dark emerald green. She had a good heart, though cloaked with mystical connections. "Are you the owner?"

Autumn walked up to the counter alongside Simone and watched the conversation unfold while staying quiet.

The woman stared at Autumn for a moment, looking deep into her eyes, and then back at Simone. "Yes, I own the apothecary. What can I do for you?"

"We're wondering about the services you offer here. I see that you have lots of tonics and potions. Is there anything for divination or enhancing psychic abilities?" Simone perused the contents of the glass counter filled with vials of strange mushrooms and barks.

Autumn's eyes wandered to a large glass jar sitting on a heat source behind the woman. A potion bubbled and steamed through the funnel opening at the top. She glimpsed shimmering purple specks of magic floating around inside the jar as it bubbled.

The woman bent down to catch Autumn's gaze from the jar. "I may have those things . . . for the right customer. Are you the right customer?" She stared directly into Autumn's hazel eyes that shifted to a deep shade of green. Taken aback, the woman stood tall. "You are." She smiled, looking between Autumn and Simone and then turning her back to gather ingredients at the counter.

Autumn and Simone exchanged confused glances. "So you have what we're looking for?" Autumn moved along the counter to see what the woman was doing.

"Please, call me Lajla." While she spoke, Lajla grabbed an eyedropper and allowed several drops of a dark-amber-colored liquid to fall into a tea mug. She crushed a few herbs in a mortar and pestle as she continued. "What shall I call you both?"

"I'm Simone, and this is my cousin, Autumn." Simone opened a few glass jars on small, round wooden tables and sniffed the contents inside. She pulled back at the powerful scents within one of them.

Lajla combined the crushed herbs into a metal tea sachet and stirred it into the mug filled with the dark liquid. She carried it over to the counter and pushed it toward Autumn. "I can help you, Autumn, but first you must drink this tea and offer me an exchange."

Simone quickly closed a wooden chest on one table and moved beside Autumn. "You mean like payment?"

Keeping her eyes on Autumn, Lajla replied, "I mean like an energy exchange. Wisdom and knowledge for a future offering of an energetic service."

Autumn looked down at the tea mug before her. She sensed the voices of her ancestors sweeping up around her. A wind howled as the front door of the shop opened, and her ancestors spoke.

"A pure source with questionable workings. A kind heart relieves all suspicions." The voices carried in Autumn's ears as the shop door knocked against the wall.

Running to close it, Lajla flipped the sign to read Closed before returning to the girls at the counter. "So is this an exchange you'd like to pursue?"

Simone cleared her throat and pulled at her cousin's sleeve. "Uh, give us a minute, would you?"

Following Simone to the side, Autumn headed over to the wall shelves and thought for a moment. "I don't think she has bad intentions."

"So you're seriously gonna drink whatever's in that mug and do an energy exchange with her?" Simone looked at Autumn like she was crazy. "That doesn't sound like my practical air energy cousin at all. What if she put something weird in that mug and she's in on all of this with someone?"

Autumn gave her cousin a relaxed smile. "You know as well as I do she doesn't have that kind of energy. She knows something, but she's not the one with the bad intentions. And I'm willing to bet an energy exchange on it."

Autumn moved her eyes from Simone to the wall behind her as she spoke. Sitting in the back corner of the wooden shelves sat a tall, skinny tonic bottle with a round stopper. The faded label on the front of the bottle carried the familiar ink stamp of a lunar eclipse. Autumn snatched the bottle from the shelf and hurried it back to the counter, positioning it beside the tea mug for Lajla to see the label.

"An energy exchange . . . Knowledge for a future offering?" Autumn stared at Lajla and waited for a reply.

Lajla nodded and gave the girls a flattened smile. "Drink, please, drink. And we shall talk."

Simone watched nervously as Autumn took several sips from the tea mug. The woman pulled out a tall, antique wooden stool from behind the counter and sat down. She straightened the fringe on the arms of her kaftan before looking up to study Autumn's eyes after the tea had been drunk.

Leaning over for a deeper look, Lajla gasped. Sapphire lights dotted Autumn's eyes and gave Lajla a glimpse into the multidimensional power Autumn held. The woman laughed under her breath and sat back on the stool. "You want to know about this bottle here?"

Simone pushed it forward toward Lajla. "Yes, what can you tell us about this tonic and the label on it?"

"Mmmm . . . Yes, it is a very interesting symbol. The lunar eclipse, just like the one that occurred several nights back." Lajla stared at Simone with a serious face and then got up to walk around the shop. "There are those who ask to connect with other worlds. With that bottle, one can open up the dream world and connect with many other dimensions, including, perhaps . . . those that are of the dark and the light."

"The dark and the light . . . From a doorway." Autumn repeated Lajla's words and recalled the voices that had come to her when she'd seen the sapphire wisps in the woods.

"You are familiar?" The woman turned to glance at Autumn as she picked up a tincture bottle from a small table. She brought the bottle back to the counter, coming around the backside to face the girls. Unscrewing the top, she pulled out an eyedropper and placed a few droplets onto a skinny strip of paper. "You asked about divination, but what you really want is the diviner." Lajla lifted her eyes to the girls as she shook the paper strip in her fingertips.

"Yes, the diviner. Do you know who we seek?" Autumn perked up and caught a whiff of mugwort from the tincture drops.

"The one who uses this bottle to reveal the secrets of their divination clients"—the apothecary owner turned the tincture bottle toward the girls—"is also the one who uses the other bottle to see worlds beyond worlds." Lajla held up the bottle with the lunar eclipse label.

"And who is that?" Autumn took another sip from the tea mug to show she would cooperate for the information.

Lajla nodded and smiled. "The bulletin board beside the front door has a full display of offerings from our community. I think if you look toward the top corner on your way out, something may pop out at you." She nodded vigorously as her tight curls bobbed up and down around her. "It was a pleasure," she said, walking toward the beaded archway. "Oh, and Autumn, I'll expect to finish our exchange on the evening of the new moon." Moving through the clattering bead chains, Lajla disappeared into the back room.

Simone and Autumn looked at each other and then raced to the front bulletin board, searching for the answer they needed.

"There!" Simone shouted. "That flier at the top is for a palm reader."

Autumn stood on her tiptoes to read the contact information on the sheet. "The future is bright with Delia in sight. Delia!"

"Wow, gag on the cheesy tagline, but it sounds like we found the right person. What's the contact info say?" Simone strained to read the flier above them.

"Uh, it says readings are available at the Hollow's Glenn downtown riverfront park on weekday evenings." Autumn fell to flat feet and smiled. "I know someone who works at the riverfront, and it's a good thing he really likes me."

CHAPTER 9

Autumn pulled the door open to the Forest Brew as the scent of Eve's apple turnovers wafted through the air. She closed her eyes for a moment and savored the smell before heading toward the counter. It was just about time for afternoon tea, and word was getting around that Eve's pastries were the best in the region. A steady stream of customers trickled in behind Autumn and quickly joined the line.

Spotting Eve pouring coffee at the side counter, Autumn lifted her hand and waved. "Hey, Eve! Are you ready?"

Eve raised her eyes to see Autumn and gave her a warm smile. "Yeah, just give me one second to wrap up." She put the coffeepot down on a towel and untied a striped linen apron around her waist.

"Take as long as you need, dear!" Mrs. Newbury walked out of the kitchen, swinging the doors behind her. "I've got lots of help today, so we should be just fine during afternoon tea." Mrs. Newbury handed Eve her toggle coat and pom knit hat before giving her a kiss on the cheek. She lingered next to Eve's ear for a moment to mention, "I'm proud of you."

Eve stepped back with a smirk as she tugged her hat over her ears. "Thanks, Mom. I'll be back as soon as I can." She grabbed a box of pastries from behind the counter and came around to meet Autumn.

"Okay, let's go." Autumn led the way toward the door. "Simone will meet us outside as soon as she finishes up with a customer at the Pine. She'll probably be done by now."

The girls angled around hungry customers edging their way into the Forest Brew for a warm treat and headed for a wooden bench on the street.

"I see Simone coming now." Eve craned her neck to look down the street.

"Good. The chief is expecting us, and it didn't sound like he had very much time. Besides, we need to keep the shop open a little longer tonight since we've been gone all day." Autumn stood up and waved at Simone as she approached them.

Simone pushed her round Lennon glasses up onto her head and sighed. "Holy moly, the paper fortunes and our popular lanterns are flying off the shelves! I had a family buy two boxes' worth of them. Plus, those new moon phase pendants are a hit!

Between the lunar eclipse and the lunar new year coming, our moon designs are a popular commodity."

"That's awesome! The Pine sounds like it's doing really well." Eve grinned and started walking toward the city hall square with the girls.

"Yeah, I'm really glad to see Main Street doing well again." Autumn pulled her knit scarf higher around her chin to keep out the chilly wind. "It was a little slow before the holidays started, but now that it's almost lunar new year, things have really picked up!"

"I think that abundance spell you did a while back may have had something to do with the traffic picking up around here, cuz." Simone smirked at Autumn.

Shrugging and crossing the street at the stoplight, Autumn shook her head at her cousin. "I simply gave things a little nudge in the right direction."

Simone laughed as they came upon Havensbrook Place and turned left. "I guess I'll believe that." She tilted her head around Eve to glimpse Autumn, who stopped to close her eyes and rub her head. Simone abruptly jolted to a stop as well. "Autumn, what is it?"

Eve huddled beside both of them on the sidewalk. "You don't look so good. Are you okay?"

"I don't . . ." Autumn stumbled back a step. "I don't know. I feel strange." She swayed slightly where she stood before collapsing to the ground.

"Autumn!" Simone grabbed her cousin, and Eve helped her lift Autumn to a bench a few paces away. "Sit down here and just breathe."

Eve placed the back of her hand on Autumn's forehead. "She's not overheated. I'm gonna unwrap her scarf a bit."

As she slowly unraveled the scarf, chimes echoed behind them from high atop the city hall bell tower. Simone and Eve peered up at the large iron bell and back down to Autumn.

Eve gasped. "Autumn's locket. I can see it glowing underneath her sweater."

Simone sat down beside her cousin and pulled on the chain around Autumn's neck to lift it from under the sweater. Eve stood directly in front of the girls to block them from passersby. As the necklace lifted higher in Simone's hands, its embossed tree root design glowed with a soft, ethereal purple hue that Simone had yet to see.

"Has it ever done that before?" Eve watched curiously.

Simone shook her head. "Not that I know of. Something's going on."

Autumn jostled around and slowly opened her eyes. "What happened?"

Simone put her chilly hand on Autumn's cheek to activate her senses. "Autumn, I think you passed out. We're next to city hall, but Eve and I are gonna help you walk around to the police station in the back, okay? They're expecting us, and we can get you warm there. Do you hear me?"

"I don't feel right. My head was spinning and then everything went fuzzy." Sitting up straighter on the bench, Autumn looked around on the busy street. "I passed out in the middle of everything?"

"Yeah, but don't worry about that now. Can you walk?" Eve tucked her head underneath Autumn's arm and lifted her slowly onto her feet while Simone supported her other side.

"I'll just go slow, okay?" Autumn turned her head to find their destination. "The police station, right? I think I can make it."

The girls walked Autumn around the corner of the stone city hall building toward the police station tucked snugly in the back corner of the square. As they pushed the front door of the station open, Simone waved to Ben at the front desk.

"What's going on?" Ben called as he rushed to help them.

They got Autumn to a black faux-leather sofa in the waiting room of the police station before her legs gave out under her.

"I just fainted, I guess. I'm not really sure." Autumn rubbed her hands down her maroon fleece leggings. "One minute we were walking down the street, heading over here, and the next minute, I couldn't focus and everything went black. And now, I feel like I've lost all my energy."

Eve, Ben, and Simone all exchanged concerned looks while a woman pushed past them with a tall glass of water.

"Here you go, love. Just drink this and you'll be as right as rain." Mavis, the older woman who worked the front desk, gave Ben a pat on the back, and winked at Simone. "A bit of mountain spring magic to do the trick," she whispered before heading back to the front desk.

Simone's mouth dropped open. She turned to Eve and shook her head. "Huh, water energy where I least expected it. You learn something new every day."

Eve chuckled and stared down at Autumn. "Eating and drinking is very grounding. That's exactly what she needs to feel better again."

"Yeah, but what caused this?" Ben crossed his arms over his chest and eyed Autumn.

"I bet it was that tea she drank from that crazy apothecary we stopped at trying to track down suspect number two." Simone caught Ben giving her the eye and then put her palm up in the air. "Don't give me that look. You know we're looking into the case, and we're fully capable of taking care of ourselves."

"You may be capable, but you don't need to take unnecessary risks. Let us handle that." Ben shook his head at her.

"Come on, you two." Autumn groaned as she pushed herself to the edge of her seat. "Stop bickering. Let's just find the chief so we can go over everything we've found."

Ben tightened his jaw and looked at Simone. "You're so stubborn, you know that?"

Flattening her lips into a smile, Simone crossed her arms to mirror his. "I could say the same about you."

"I've been waiting for all of you," the chief's voice chimed in from behind the front desk. "Why don't you all come to the conference room, and we'll talk. Follow me."

Ben helped the girls get Autumn to the conference room, and they all grabbed a chair around the table before the chief started again.

"Sorry I wasn't out front to meet you right away. There was a break-in at the lawyer's office in town, and I sent several officers over there. The place was covered with mud and rocks, so we needed to collect samples of everything. It's been a busy morning." Chief Walsh took the seat at the head of the table and looked around the room. "Now, what's the latest you've found on Ayla's case?"

Autumn propped her forearms onto the table and leaned in. "Chief, we're concerned about some news Eve heard over at the Forest Brew."

"Oh yeah? About what?" Ian Walsh turned to Eve at the end of the table.

Eve smoothed her dark-blonde hair away from her face and cleared her throat. "Well, I always overhear people talking in the coffee shop, and this time it was about Brodie Aitken, Ayla's ex-husband."

"Ah, Brodie." The chief sat back in his chair and shared a glance with Ben, as if they both knew a backstory. "I haven't seen him around these parts in quite some time. Not sure if he's officially Ayla's ex-husband, but I know they've had their fair share of problems over the years. What've you heard?"

"Well, from all the talk at the Forest Brew, he's back in town and moving back home. Several people heard him talking about how he's coming back to Ayla." Eve folded her hands together in her lap and waited patiently for a response.

"Hmm, Brodie Aitken back in Hollow's Glenn. Well, that is news to me. I know the Blake County Sheriff's Department gathered all their evidence from Ayla's property and opened up the scene, so I suppose he has the right to stay on the premises. As far as I know, Ayla and Brodie never formally divorced, so I don't think we'd have cause to make him vacate the home, if that is in fact where he's staying. But, if I know Brodie, there's trouble following him. And it is awfully suspicious that he returned right after Ayla went missing." Chief Walsh turned toward his son. "Ben, let's follow up on this and see if we can find out what Brodie's up to. What else have you got, girls?"

"We talked to the people over at the fairgrounds in Blake County. Turns out there were a couple people who may have had it out for Ayla." Simone glanced at Ben as he gave her a disapproving look. She shrugged at him and whispered, "What?"

"All right, I'm listening." The chief leaned his swivel chair closer to the table. "Who are these people?"

"The first was a man who burst into one of the Lunar Fest meetings and yelled at Ayla." Autumn recalled what Mr. Doyle had told the girls. "It was something about a tarot reading she gave to his relative, and it turned out the man lost his inheritance because of it. That one sounded like it could turn into something serious."

"Get a name on the guy?" the chief questioned.

Autumn shook her head. "No, but we could track down a list of Ayla's clients and go from there."

"Okay, let's stay on that one." Chief Walsh turned to Ben, who was already writing the details of Autumn's description. "What about the other potential suspect?"

"Delia Hall." Simone said the words with distrust in her tone. "A local palm reader who seems to be a bit shady."

"Tell me more." The chief raised his chin at Simone.

Tilting her head, trying to figure out where to begin, Simone sighed. "Apparently she's into using potions to get ahead with her clients and whatever else she's into. The festival chair said she's been gunning for Ayla's booth for years and has been very pushy about it all of a sudden."

"That's right," Autumn continued. "They hadn't even publicized that the booth was available since Ayla's been missing. Delia may have already known that it was the opportune time to grab it. Not to mention, having that booth is a big bonus this year, with a large publishing house coming to town to strike a book deal. It would be the perfect way to scale a fortune-telling business."

"So she definitely had a motive to get Ayla out of the picture." Ben jotted down a few more details into his notebook. "Still, none of this tells us why Autumn found the dead neighbor on the property."

"Could be the wrong place at the wrong time." Ian Walsh looked at his son, trying to piece the clues together. "But I don't know if that fits. There's something more we're missing." He perked up and quieted his voice. "Which reminds me . . . These strange lights that people have been seeing around the mountain region. Do you girls know anything about them?"

Autumn, Simone, and Eve all looked at each other in confusion. Autumn came back to the chief and read a sense of concern coming over him.

"We don't know what they are, but . . ." Autumn glanced at Simone and then back at the chief. "It's possible that Simone and I saw some the other day."

Chief Walsh leaned back in his chair and swiveled around, thinking. "Let me guess, right by your cottage?"

"That's right. How did you know, Chief?" Simone peered at him in interest.

"Someone else saw them, too," Autumn interjected without hesitation. She inherently knew that whatever lay within the woods near Mrs. Pendleton's cottage drew closer by the day. And she wasn't sure whether it would bring light or dark.

CHAPTER 10

Simone grabbed the steaming tea mug from the back-office counter at Parchment and Pine and brought it to Autumn sitting in the hearth room. Autumn kicked her boots off to the side and tucked her legs underneath her in the wingback chair beside the fireplace.

"Thanks," Autumn said, grabbing the hot mug from Simone. Tavish circled on the floor next to the fire and plopped down with his tail curled around him. "I'm feeling better."

"Good, but don't push it. I don't want you keeling over on me again." Simone pointed straight at her cousin as she turned to walk out of the archway. "It was hard enough lifting you the first time."

The front door chime rang, and their mothers rushed into the shop. "Oh, girls!" Jo scurried across the floor toward the hearth room. "There you are! Catherine Newbury called the store a moment ago. Eve told her that Autumn collapsed this afternoon, and she got us all worried! How are you, dear?"

Simone rolled her eyes at her mother. "I'll boil more water."

Penny strolled in and patted Simone on the shoulder. "Thank you, my dear." She went to check on her daughter beside the fire. "Autumn, tell us what happened." She put a hand to Autumn's forehead and nodded in approval.

"I'm okay. It's fine. I just felt strange on our way to the police station today. When we got to city hall square, suddenly my energy completely faded. Everything got fuzzy, and I must have passed out." Autumn wrapped her hands around the warm mug of chamomile tea and took a sip.

Penny and Jo exchanged knowing glances. "So you say you were in city hall square?" Penny swallowed hard.

"It had to have been from this crazy tea Autumn drank earlier today," Simone called, walking through the shop with a large tray full of mugs. "I told her not to, but she seemed to think it was a good idea."

Penny shook her head, grabbed a cup of tea, and turned her back to face the fire. "No, my dears. I don't think it was tea that did this."

"Although, we should discuss that tea in a moment," Jo said with seriousness in her voice.

"It's the bell, isn't it?" Autumn looked up at Aunt Jo, waiting for an answer.

Jo gave her a sympathetic look. "Yes, dear. It's the bell. When did you start noticing it?"

"The bell? What do you mean? The big bell tower at city hall?" Simone peeked her head out of the archway to see if any customers were inside the shop and then brought her focus back to Autumn. "How could the bell be a problem?"

"I can't describe it, but for a few months now, I've sensed a heavy energy the closer I've gotten to city hall. And I assumed that they'd just recently installed the bell since I had never seen it before, although I know I've always heard the chimes." Autumn stared at Jo and her mother, confused.

"We meant for the spell to protect you from it." Penny turned around with tears in her eyes. "The cloaking spell your gran had done."

"Cloaking spell? Why would you need a cloaking spell for a bell?" Simone sat down on the floor beside Autumn and sipped her own tea.

Trying to make sense of her mother's words, Autumn looked into the fire as the insight came to her. "Because it could hurt me."

"That's right, love. The bell was forged of iron, and the town raised it for protection when a dark illness spread over the lands. The bell blocked foreign energies and kept our people safe, but . . . you have some of that energy within you." Penny sat down at the base of the fireplace and placed her hand over

Autumn's on the arm of the chair. "It's an energy from your father."

Autumn's eyes darted up to meet her mother's. "My father? Who is he and what kind of energy are you talking about?"

Jo and Simone exchanged glances. "Penny, do you want Simone and me to give you some privacy?" Jo suggested.

Penny shook her head and stretched her legs out under her long, thick skirt. "No, we're all in this together, and we'll find a solution together." She sighed and continued. "Autumn, your father was a fae. You have witch blood from the MacKinnons, but you are also half fae."

Autumn laughed out loud. "I'm a fairy? How is that possible? You've never talked about any of this before."

"That's because we thought that world remained lost to us . . . and your father along with it. With the frost sickness, we had to block the portal to their lands, and I feared the worst as the dark fae spread the frost." Penny sniffed and took a sip of tea for comfort. "I knew there would come a day when you would discover who you really are. That tree root charm I gave you that now fused to your gran's necklace . . . Your father, Laith, originally charged it with protective fae energy. You carry his energy with you now, and that of his people."

"Laith . . ." Autumn pulled the locket from under her soft white sweater and turned it in her fingers.

"It glowed with a purplish hue earlier at city hall. Eve and I both saw it," Simone confirmed.

Jo nodded and sank into the other wingback chair opposite Autumn. She smoothed her velvet skirt over her lap and smiled. "Purple signals the spiritual connection between worlds. A higher level of energy than that surrounding us here, although it can be dark as well."

"The light and the dark," Autumn whispered.

"Yes," Penny confirmed. "And the worlds have blurred, which is why we had to raise the iron bell for protection. Iron shields from the fae energy. They cannot go near it, and neither can you, my dear, unless we cloak it from you." She looked at her daughter and grabbed her hand once again. "And we will see to that again."

"I don't understand. This is a lot to process." Autumn ran her hand over her face. "You're telling me I'm the four-points witch along with having fae blood, but iron is my kryptonite. Oh, and by the way, I've been living and working down the street from it my whole life."

Jo and Penny laughed as the front doorbell chimed. Simone stood up to see Eve walking through the door. Waving her back, Simone pulled the heavy curtains that lined the hearth room archway open a bit more.

"Come on in, Eve. We're just talking about how Autumn is actually part fae." Simone put a hand on her hip.

"Are you serious?" Eve quickened her pace to the hearth room. "That means you have stronger earth energy than we thought! Wait . . . The lights! The lights around town that you both saw near your cottage. There's a portal there, isn't there?"

Autumn and Simone exchanged glances, finally putting the pieces together. "They were in the woods between Gran's house and Mrs. Pendleton's. Did you both know about this?" Autumn turned to Jo and Penny.

Jo dipped her middle finger into her tea mug to make ripples in the water. "Hawthorn Cottage." A likeness of the cottage appeared in the ripples of her mug as she spoke. "The hawthorn tree serves as a portal between worlds. It's greatly revered for its energy of connection, protection, and love. Your gran hoped that tree would thrive on the land for generations."

"She knew? You all knew?" Simone squinted her eyes at her mother.

"And the wisps?" Autumn interjected.

Eve gasped and covered her mouth with her hands, jumping up and down. "You've seen wisps? This is incredible!"

"You never told me you saw the wisps. When was this?" Penny stood to top off her mug with more hot water from the teapot on the table.

"I saw them once when I was a child. The little sapphire colors twinkled and danced around like fireflies, but I had no idea what they were. They beckoned me toward them, though, and I found their mushroom circle at the base of the hawthorn tree. But then, just the other day, they appeared again." Autumn looked up at Aunt Jo for an answer to why.

Jo swirled her tea with her finger, and tiny golden shimmers rose from her cup. "The lunar eclipse creates powerful water energy to open worlds usually unseen."

"Earth energy benefitting from the power of water." Eve turned toward Simone. "But do they create chaos or order?"

Simone raised her eyebrows and followed Eve's train of thought. "Darkness or light? I think we should find out this evening at the downtown park. There's a shady fortune teller who may just have the answer to that."

CHAPTER 11

Simone locked the front door of Parchment and Pine for the night and lifted the collar on her quilted coat. She turned to head out with Autumn beside her and Tavish tucked snuggly into his flannel-lined carrier.

"Are you sure you're okay to be walking down Main Street? After you collapsed today, I don't think you should go anywhere near that bell." Simone raised her eyebrows at her cousin as they passed the flower shop next door and waved to Mrs. Leslie through the well-adorned window.

"Sim, I'll be fine. I go down to the Forest Brew all the time, and nothing's happened to me over there. You don't have to worry about me, although I appreciate it." Autumn gave her cousin a slight smile as they crossed the street and headed for Jo's bath shop.

"Yeah, but Gran's spell is fading by the day. You heard your mom. You need to be careful around that iron until we can perform a new spell to keep you safe. So quit trying to look out for everyone but yourself. It's time we looked after you." Simone yanked on the bath shop door, and beautiful scents of citrus and vanilla wafted through at them.

Autumn made her way inside, with Tavish jumping out of his carrier to find Aunt Jo as soon as he sensed where he was. The cat always loved a warm welcome from her that usually included a bit of his favorite treats.

Jo crossed the shop floor and snatched Tavish up into her arms. "There's my little taste tester. I think I have some poached salmon in the back for you tonight." Jo took the cat to the back room as the girls found Penny in the seating area on the far wall.

"Ah, girls." Penny rose from reading on the sofa. "Right on time for us to cat-sit that little one." Penny clasped her hands together and looked at her daughter. "Now, Autumn, are you sure you're feeling up for heading down to the river-front tonight? You could just as easily let James check out this palm reader on his own, or Simone could go eavesdrop along with him."

Autumn shook her head. "No, Mom, I'm fine. I already told Simone that I'll be all right. I won't go directly near city hall, so there won't be a problem, even if the cloaking spell wears off a bit. The riverfront sits far enough away that I should still have my energy."

Penny shifted her worried gaze between the girls. "Well, all right, if you think you're up to it. We really need to find out as much as we can and soon. Ayla's been gone for a couple days now, and I don't want her to end up like that poor neighbor of hers."

"I know, Mom. We'll find her." Autumn placed her hand gently on her mother's arm. "And we've gotta figure out how this neighbor, Philip Gibson, got involved. I know he wasn't over there just as a concerned neighbor looking out for Ayla. There's definitely something more to it."

"Let's just start with who we know wanted Ayla out of the picture, and then we can figure out how this neighbor fits in." Simone's words faded as a late customer flew into the shop.

"Welcome to Calming Moon Bath and Body!" Jo's voice called out from the back of the store. "I'll be right with you."

Penny walked over to the customer and took her hands. "Fiona Miller. How are you, my darling?"

Fiona smiled warmly at Penny and then embraced her in a hug. "Oh, it's so lovely to see you, Penny! It's been ages!"

"Yes, it's been far too long. But you know, this is the perfect opportunity to invite you to the tea party I'll be hosting tomorrow evening at the house. I'm doing a monthly tea to celebrate taking over my late mother's tea business. You simply must come so we can catch up!"

"Oh, that would be lovely, Penny! I'll be there with bells on!" Fiona smiled warmly, and Simone watched as an aura of teal blue came over the old friends.

Jo came to the front of the shop to join the older ladies in their reunion. "Why, Fiona Miller! What are you doing in Hollow's Glenn? Testing the waters to see when the lake is ready for a swim?" Jo put her arm around Fiona and turned her toward Autumn and Simone. "Girls, Fiona used to be my toughest competition in the mountain region swim meets."

Swatting her hand through the air in dismissal, Fiona shook her head at the comment. "Oh, nonsense, Josephine. You were always the one on top of the boards for swimming those meters. Anyway, I'm here on the suggestion of a mutual friend."

"Oh? What suggestion is that?" Jo brushed a loose strand of hair back into her crown braids and put her hands on her hips.

"Well, I was just telling Ayla Ross this morning about my terrible insomnia, and—"

"Ayla?" The four other ladies cut Fiona off in unison.

Taken aback by the sudden question, Fiona hesitated. "Yes, Sorcha and Dillon's sister, Ayla. You know we've been close over the years."

Jo took Fiona's elbow and dragged her over to the side sofa to sit. "Yes, yes, we know, Fiona. But how could you have seen Ayla this morning? She's been missing for days."

"Missing? That's impossible! She stood right before me at the market in Ivansedge, just buying some melons and bread." Fiona motioned with her hands as she spoke.

"And she spoke with you about your insomnia?" Autumn squinted at the woman, getting a sense for whether her energy seemed reliable.

"Yes, we stood in line at the checkout counter, and I mentioned having such terrible insomnia lately. So, she recommended a lavender bath before bed. And you know, the Rosses have always been so gifted in dreamwork that I just took her word as truth. I mean, this morning she went on and on about how my insomnia could be related to unresolved issues, or perhaps some messages needed to come through to me in my wake state. But Ayla was adamant that lavender would enhance my sleep and put me in touch with more relaxed realms. That's when I remembered you had this lovely bath shop here in Hollow's Glenn, and I knew I needed to come see my dear friend Josephine." Fiona slapped her palms down on her thighs. "Now, how can I get some of your lovely lavender bath salts, Jo? I'm so eager to try them tonight."

Jo looked over at the girls' faces in astonishment and then returned to the matter at hand. "All right, I have some lavender vanilla salts that I mixed up recently. Meet me at the back counter, and I'll scoop some into a jar for you." Jo led Fiona to the back of the shop while Penny, Autumn, and Simone eyed each other, dumbfounded.

"So did Ayla just skip town for a couple days and then come back?" Simone slid down onto the couch beside Penny.

Tavish wandered up toward Autumn, pausing at her feet to give himself a bath after what seemed like a good meal.

She scooped up the cat and fell into the side chair to let her thoughts come to her. "What do you think, Tav? Does it make sense that Ayla's back?" She rubbed the cat's belly as he'd allow only her to do, and an insight came to her mind. "That lunar eclipse symbol is coming to mind over and over again. Something is leading me back to the moon."

Simone leaned in close and whispered, "Do you think Ayla is into some kind of weird moon magic? I mean, after what we've been through with all the black magic the past few months, I wouldn't put it past anyone to have some skeletons hidden in their closets." Simone shrugged and shook her head. "I'm just saying."

"No, Ayla would never dabble in anything dark." Penny rose from the sofa and began pacing the floor. "I've known the entire Ross family my whole life, and Ayla always carried an ethereal grace to her. She was well-connected to other realms, as one who astral projects, after all. But never have I known her energy to seek anything but a high vibration."

"Well, we need to keep an open mind here." Autumn put Tavish down on the couch and pulled her maroon slouchy knit hat from her backpack. "Nothing is beyond possibility. If I've learned anything since Gran's passing, it's that the world is not as it seems."

The three of them looked up as Jo led Fiona to the door and waved goodbye. Josephine turned to them all getting up from their places and moving toward her. "Oh, I missed the conversation! What do you all sense?"

Autumn tugged on her hat and adjusted her backpack. "That the moon is the culprit in all of this. I'm just not sure how."

"Hey, don't blame the water energy of the moon! It's my one true love!" Simone smirked as she wrapped a charcoal-colored scarf around her neck. "Besides, I think someone's manipulating us somehow. Playing games with this disappearance and then reappearance. Moon energy usually hints at things under the surface, you know."

Jo nodded and held the door open for the girls. "Simone is right. Nothing is certain when it comes to the moon. You must be on your toes and willing to go with anything that comes to the surface." Jo kissed Simone's cheek and put her hand on Autumn's arm. "Be careful around this palm reader tonight, girls. Keep James close by, and if you feel any sign of alarm, heed the warning and get out of there."

Chapter 12

Autumn gently pressed the door closed on the passenger side of Simone's black Jeep SUV and headed down the grassy hill toward the riverfront. She spotted James on the construction site where his father's company worked to revitalize the riverfront area. James spoke with a few workers who were placing cobblestones on a path leading toward the historic water fountain, one Autumn's Gran fought vigorously to maintain in her time.

James caught Autumn's eye and waved. He nodded to the man beside him and handed him a clipboard. Zipping his work jacket up to the collar and shoving his hands down into his jeans, James walked up the hill toward Autumn and Simone. "Evening, ladies."

"Hey, stranger." Autumn smiled at him. "Thanks for doing this for us."

He sighed and looked down the park a ways into the dark. "You say she's in the pavilion on the other side of the fountain?"

Autumn looked in that same direction. "Yeah, she'll probably take readings there for the next hour. All you need to do is ask for a palm reading and see if you can get any information about the festival and her connection to Ayla."

"Keep your eyes open, though," Simone interjected. "We were told she's got some less than ethical techniques, so don't let her scam you."

"Right. She may try to use some potions or something for the reading. If you can catch her with some, though, that might be an opportunity to discover her methods and find out what else she might be into." Autumn put her hands on his chest and pressed her lips gently onto his. "Be careful. We don't know what she's capable of."

James looked at her with his warm brown eyes. "Oh, she won't try anything out here in the public park. There're too many workers still out, and no one would be stupid enough to cause a scene."

As the words left James's mouth, Autumn squinted as something shiny caught the streetlight behind him. The light drew her eye up the hill at the edge of the street, where she spotted a familiar-looking man in a tailored wool coat. The hint of shininess peeked out from his coat sleeve as he pulled a small manila envelope out of the car door and tucked it under his arm before walking into the park.

"That's the man we saw rushing out of the fairgrounds office." Autumn stared at him curiously as James and Simone did the same.

"You're right." Simone nodded. "What's he doing all the way out here? Getting a palm reading?"

James turned toward the girls and shook off the man. "Let's just focus on what we came for. You both stay here while I go get that reading."

"All right, Simone and I will wait on our gran's bench by the waterfront just in case. Come find us when you're done." Autumn brushed her hand across his jawline and smiled before walking away toward the bench with Simone.

Simone leaned in close to her cousin and whispered, "Are you getting the sense that he'll be successful?"

Autumn lifted a brow as she sat and rubbed her hand over the nameplate dedicated to her gran on the bench. "I know he'll come back with something, but I'm getting the idea that it'll create more questions than answers."

James hovered near the river as he approached the pavilion where the palm reader gave readings. He eyed her as an older woman nervously sat down across from her at the table. Once she sat, he recognized the woman to be a stingy lady for whom he once did a renovation project. She had always been uptight and rigid about every aspect of that project.

The reader took the woman's money and then pulled out a small bottle under the table. She removed a dropper and allowed a substance to drip onto her fingertip while she closed her eyes. Proceeding to start the reading, she grabbed the woman's palm and ran her finger along the length of it before starting.

Wanting to get a closer look without seeming curious, James meandered toward the pavilion as though he were just waiting for his chance at a reading. His eyes wandered over the wooden A-frame signs displaying the divination prices on either side of Delia's table, and then he brought his attention back to her.

"Oh my word!" exclaimed the older woman. "Can you see more?"

Delia squinted at the woman's hand and drew it closer while shaking her head. Then, she pulled the crystal ball beside her closer to the center of the table and encouraged the woman to add onto her reading.

"Yes, yes, of course!" The woman couldn't get her pocketbook out fast enough to hand over the money for the crystal ball.

As the two women sat on either side of the crystal, James watched deep-purple shimmers fly within it. He wondered if the older woman could see what he saw. Either way, he got the feeling that the palm reader played with magic beyond her own capabilities.

The older woman's reading finished, and she turned to walk away as she glanced at James waiting nearby. "Oh, she's worth every penny!" She swatted the air as she spoke. "Just go for the full package. You won't be sorry."

James smiled at her and nodded. "Glad you had a good reading, ma'am." He took a seat at the palm reader's table as the other woman walked away.

Delia Hall glared at him from across the table and looked him up and down. "You'd like a reading?"

"Yes, I'm interested in getting a head start for the new year, as there's a lot going on. So, I'll take a palm reading, please." He pulled some money from his wallet and placed it on the table.

Immediately taking the money and sliding it under the table, Delia glanced up at him again. "My name is Delia, and I've been doing divination for many years. Some say it is in my blood." She fiddled with a few things under the table that James assumed included the small bottle he had seen earlier. "I just need to prepare my energy before the reading." She closed her eyes and rubbed her hands together.

As she opened them, she held her hands out on the table. "Now, we can begin. Hands, please."

James hesitated, knowing that whatever substance Delia had marked the older woman's hands with had made her a very open and willing customer, something he knew her not to be. "Actually, I have a hangup about other people touching me . . . Germs, and all. Can I just lay my palm here on the table for you to see?"

She eyed him with suspicion and thought for a moment as he flattened his hand. "Palm reading works best if I can follow the lines with my fingers and feel the energy."

"Maybe it's better that I stick to a tarot reading, then. I'll just take my money back and then—" He stood up from the table as Delia stopped him abruptly.

"No! No, please, sit." She motioned her hands to signal him to sit back down. "We will do a reading from the crystal ball instead. Same price, but please, sit."

James sat down again, adjusting his work jacket and warming his hands in his pockets. "Thank you. I really appreciate it, as I'd really like to know about the new year."

Delia grabbed the heavy crystal ball from beside her and placed it in the center of the table. A purple cloud covered the inside of the ball and gave it an almost opaque hue. She grabbed for something else beneath the table, rubbing her hands together again. Then, while swirling her hands over the crystal, she asked, "What is it you seek?"

"There's a relationship in my life. I'm curious if it will develop further this year." James swallowed hard with actual sincerity in his question. He wondered whether Delia had enough real magic within her to give him a solid answer.

After he spoke his intention, the cloud within the ball dissipated. Delia swirled her hands faster around it and hummed softly, as if coaxing something out of the cloud. Deep-purple shimmers appeared under the crystal surface, and the interior of the ball became more translucent.

James squinted his eyes to look within it to find an emblem marking the base of the ball. Appearing under the purple shimmers sat the same lunar eclipse symbol found on the papers in Ayla's home.

"It's the same," he murmured under his breath.

"The same?" Delia eyed him, curiously.

He shook himself out of his thoughts and back to focus on the palm reader. "Oh, I was thinking . . ."—he tried coming up with something that would make sense to cover his findings—"that this works the same as the crystal ball reading I had when I was younger."

"Mmmm . . . Divination through scrying can take many forms, but I find the crystal ball to be consistent. Now, about your year ahead." She swirled her hands around the ball some more as the shimmers danced inside the crystal. "I see that whomever it is you speak of also has a great fondness for you. However, some family issues for this person must come first. Thus, the coming months require space, but stay present and available for a longer relationship to come."

Delia pulled a drinking glass from a container under the table. She placed it under a water dispenser beside the table and slowly tilted the spout open to fill the glass. James watched as hints of dark-purple shimmers circled inside the water.

"Here," she said, handing him the glass. "Drink this to clarify the reading and your thoughts."

James glanced down at the glass and tilted his head. Nothing about this woman said "trustworthy" to James, and he wasn't about to take anything she gave him. "That's all right. I've got my water down at the restoration site on the river. I appreciate the reading, though. If I have more questions, will you be at the Lunar Fest?" He needed to find out a bit more before leaving.

"Why, yes, it turns out that I'll have a very prominent booth at the festival this year. You'll easily be able to find me for a second reading. Plus, I have a feeling I'll be coming out with a book very soon." Delia started cleaning off her crystal ball with a cloth while she spoke.

"Oh? A book?" James watched as the purple cloud reemerged within the ball as she cleaned it.

"That's right. An opportunity has presented itself, and I'm going to be expanding my business this year. So, if you'd like another reading or you're interested in the book, then just take one of my cards on the edge of the table. I always have openings for readings." She smirked at him as he got up and took one of her cards.

James waved the card in the air. "Thanks. I'll keep that in mind." He raised his finger with a thought. "Oh, and do you by any chance do any . . . moon work?"

She stopped cleaning the crystal ball and looked straight into his eyes. "Moon work? What is it you're looking for, exactly?"

"For manifesting or maybe dreamwork?" He shrugged, keeping his hands in his pockets and offering an innocent expression. "I mean, I think I could use all the help I can get at making this a good year, and I've just heard that the moon can be very good for working on what you want. You know, we just had that crazy lunar eclipse, so I figured maybe the moon could help me out. Do you do any of that?"

Delia cleared her throat and sat up straight, eyeing another customer in the distance. "It's possible that moon work can be done . . . for a price. You have my card. Contact me if there is a specific need that arises. Now, I must attend to my next customer." She waved the next person toward her and took their money straight away.

James smiled and waved her card in the air again. "Right, thanks again for the reading." He walked toward the river and back to the girls at Gran's bench, while going over the divination reading in his mind.

As soon as Autumn saw him coming, she stood up, sensing the uneasiness in his energy. She waited for him to get closer before asking, "What did you find out?"

Simone stood as well and glanced at his muddy red aura. "She creeped you out, didn't she?"

James ran a hand over his forehead. "Yeah, that was weird. Can we just sit by the water for a minute? I need to shake off some of that strange energy."

The girls nodded and followed James over to the riverfront. They crossed the walking path and took a few steps onto the grass that lined the water's edge. James sat down and wrapped his arms around his knees.

Sighing, he looked at the two of them. "Delia's definitely not completely legit, although I think she does have some insight. She's using something to enhance it, though. I saw her pulling out a small glass bottle before the readings. I think she rubbed some kind of substance on a woman's hand, and it must have gotten her to open up, because I knew that woman. She'd never have been so willing to hand over money like I saw."

Autumn and Simone glanced at each other with knowing. "The tinctures," they said simultaneously.

Placing a hand on James's arm, Autumn turned to him. "She must have used the tinctures from the apothecary. We think they make people very receptive and accommodating, perhaps to the point of paying for services they don't really want and being really forthcoming with giving information during the readings."

James chuckled under his breath. "Yeah, that makes sense. Good thing I didn't let her use any of the potions on me. I had a feeling she was up to something. But the thing that concerned me most was . . ." He paused as a small wave pushed along the river's edge and broke the calm of the water.

The girls waited patiently for him to continue. Autumn bit her lip, considering what he would say next that might give another clue to Ayla's disappearance or Mr. Gibson's death.

"I found the lunar eclipse symbol inside her crystal ball. The same symbol that we've been seeing sat at the base of the crystal. There was a deep-purple haze that cleared from it, and as it faded, I could see the symbol at the bottom. Plus, she seemed very apprehensive when I asked if she did any moon work." He watched the river calm down once more and flow gently away from them.

"She's definitely into something. Whether or not this is about Ayla, that woman has an agenda." Simone scooted down by the water, pushed her coat sleeves up, and dipped her hands in. She let the cold energy of it wash over her arms as she spun her hand in a small circle. Hints of golden shimmers formed at the water's edge, and a little whirlpool developed in front of her.

"Oh yeah. After my reading, she mentioned getting the booth at the Lunar Fest. She appeared pretty happy about it and even mentioned a book coming out soon." James watched Simone play with the whirlpool of water, and Autumn sensed his energy calming to a more peaceful state.

"That must be the book deal Ayla intended to get from the publisher at the festival. So, now that Ayla's out of the picture, Delia has a wide-open opportunity to get the book deal instead. She's definitely at the top of our suspect list. Now, we just have to figure out her whereabouts the night of the lunar eclipse." Autumn rubbed James's back beside her. "Thank you for doing this for us. I know it's hard to be around someone's toxic energy, especially with so much water energy in you. Why don't you dip your hands into the whirlpool with Simone?" She encouraged him with a smile. "The water will cleanse any of the residual energy away that you may have absorbed."

James nodded and kissed Autumn's cheek. He looked into her hazel eyes and watched glints of light pink sparkle for a moment. "She wasn't completely off, though. Some things are worth the wait."

Unsure of what he meant, Autumn smiled at him with curiosity as he moved over to the water's edge and dipped his hands into the whirlpool. Simone spun her hands around a few times more to keep it going for him, and his aura turned back to its normal shade of powder blue.

CHAPTER 13

The next afternoon the waning moon had already started making its way into the sky before the sun had set. Penny, Autumn, and Simone finished decorating the back garden at Jo's house by sprinkling fresh iris petals on the farm table. The iris flowers had been one of Gran's favorites, and since this new monthly tea party marked the continuation of Gran's tea business, Penny wanted to bring her energy to the event.

Walking to the side wall of the house, Penny touched the soil of the garden bed. She smoothed her hand over the dirt and whispered a few words under her breath, lifting her hands into the air as she spoke. As her hands rose, sprouts followed them up and quickly grew into tall iris flowers with bluish-purple hues.

Autumn walked over and wrapped her arms tightly around her mother's shoulders. "Those look beautiful, Mom. Gran would be very happy."

Penny kissed her daughter's forehead and smiled. "I think you're right. It makes me happy to think she may be here to enjoy this with us, too."

"She is!" Simone piped up from pouring water into large glass bowls along the center of the table. "I sensed her energy next to you a minute ago." Simone continued to place a few floating flower petals and votive candles into the water bowls.

"Yeah, and a memory just popped into my mind of when Gran planted some irises along the path to my sanctuary woods. She said she wanted to brighten the way to my favorite spot in the trees. I guess Gran wants us all to know she's here to celebrate with us today." Autumn flipped the switch on the outer wall and watched the Edison bulbs light up the trees in the garden.

"Oh, girls! I'm just so excited for this new endeavor!" Penny stared hopefully at the beautifully set garden table as she spoke. "I've been thinking . . . To reinvent the tea collection Gran started, I want to expand it into a whole line of holistic healing remedies. You got me thinking about it the other day when you went to that apothecary. So, I spoke to my dear friend from the founding families, Rose Carmichael. Since she oversees the hospital, I wanted her take on this, and well . . . she didn't know why I had waited so long!"

Josephine pushed through the back door of the house, carrying two large jugs of water with sliced oranges floating over ice. "What's all this about healing remedies I'm sensing?" She placed the jugs in between the floating candle displays on the table and stood to admire the decor. "Lovely."

"Aunt Penny wants to expand the teas into a holistic remedy collection. It sounds amazing!" Simone helped her mother put teacups at each place setting on the table.

"Oh, she finally said something! I was beginning to think I would have to keep that to myself for another year!" Jo pressed her palms to her cheeks and shook her head. "Pen, I'm so glad you're finally doing this!"

Penny buttoned half of her olive-green cable-knit cardigan and put her hands on the hips of her plaid wool skirt. "Josephine MacKinnon, you knew? You knew I planned to expand the business, and you didn't ask me about it?" She leaned a hand onto a wooden keyhole-back dining chair and gave her sister the eye.

Jo chuckled as she folded napkins into quarters. "Of course I knew. The moment you told me you planned to continue our mother's tea business with a more healing approach, my intuition told me you'd grow it into something more. I'm just glad the day is finally here that you're fully embracing it. Now, the guests should arrive any minute."

A meow interjected the conversation as Tavish pushed his way through the cat door at the back of the house. He trotted up to Autumn and rubbed against her leg.

"Looks like someone's ready to be social." Autumn bent down and scooped up the cat just as footsteps turned the corner on the wraparound porch.

"Hello!" Mrs. Leslie walked down the porch steps into the garden. She hugged Penny and smiled warmly. "Oh, Penny, this is lovely! And those iris flowers!" Karen Leslie gasped. "I don't even have irises available in the flower shop yet! How in the world did you get those to bloom so early? We've only just started February!"

Penny smiled and patted Karen's shoulders. "The ones in this garden seem to love showing up early! Please, have a seat. The afternoon tea will be ready shortly."

Several ladies, including Sorcha Allan, Rose Carmichael, Cornelia Lachlan, and Mrs. Pendleton, showed up, making their way to the garden table. Autumn and Simone brought out small teapots containing Penny's new tea blends, along with platters of cranberry orange scones and clotted cream from the Forest Brew.

Eve and her mother scurried around the porch next, carrying another trayful of caramelized pear tartlets with them. "We made it! Sorry for the delay!" Mrs. Newbury called as she rushed to place the tartlets in the center of the table. "Oh, how wonderful is all of this?"

Autumn waved for Eve to come sit at the other end of the table by her and Simone as Jo and Penny greeted Mrs. Newbury. Lainy walked straight through the back door of the house into the garden and flopped directly into a chair beside Eve.

"Hey." Lainy sighed, unraveling her camel coat to reveal a sleek black turtleneck sweater underneath. "It feels good out here this afternoon. I've been cooped up in city hall all day trying to plan some kind of retirement ceremony for Chief Walsh."

"Retirement ceremony?" Jo's ears perked up at the mention of Chief Walsh. "He's retiring so soon? I thought he'd have at least another couple years in him."

Lainy shook her head. "Nope. I guess the case he's working on now has him ready to call it quits." The hint of the case made Sorcha uneasy at the other end of the table, and Jo leaned over to place a hand on her arm. Lainy continued as she grabbed a scone off a tray. "From what I hear, there'll be a vote in the next couple months about the chief's replacement." She met eyes with Simone across the table from her. "All signs point to Ben at this point. There's no reason to believe it'll be anyone else."

Mrs. Leslie cleared her throat at the center of the table and poured from the apple chai teapot. "Well, since we're sharing the town chatter and mentioning the latest news, I have been hearing some things in the flower shop lately. Just this morning Mrs. Aitken came in from Blake County and went on about her oldest boy, Brodie, being back in the region."

Sorcha's hand shook at hearing his name, and her tea splashed out from her teacup. Jo quickly brought a napkin toward her and helped clean up the mess.

"Brodie, Ayla's husband?" Sorcha asked nervously.

Mrs. Leslie paused for a moment. "Yes, dear. From what I gather, he and his brother, Dunn, have been bickering quite a bit lately. Apparently Ayla did a tarot reading for Mrs. Aitken, her mother-in-law, who then cut Dunn out of his inheritance for her property. The boys are driving her crazy going at it daily about the property rights, and they've been at each other's throats as well. She wanted to brighten up her days and take her mind off it all with some flowers from the shop."

"So, Dunn is Ayla's brother-in-law?" Autumn chimed in to make sense of what Mrs. Leslie was confirming.

"That's right, dear." Sorcha looked down at her plate as she spoke. "I've been telling my sister for years that Brodie is no good, and neither's his brother. She refused to listen until several months ago when she finally kicked Brodie out of the house. I don't think Ayla finalized the divorce papers until very recently, though, but that family gave her nothing but heartache all these years. I'm not surprised to hear those boys are doing the same thing to their mother."

Eve snatched a cranberry orange scone and tore a piece off the edge. She whispered to the girls beside her. "Ayla finalized her divorce papers. That probably didn't make Brodie happy either."

Autumn nodded as she poured from the vanilla rooibos teapot. "You're right, Eve. That's an interesting development. If Dunn was the one upset with Ayla about the tarot reading that lost his inheritance, then he must have been the one to storm into the Lunar Fest meeting yelling at Ayla. And then, there's Brodie. He could have come back to town to convince her not to file for divorce. But, if it already went through . . ."

Lainy leaned in close and kept her tone quiet. "He may have gotten angry enough to do something drastic."

"Drastic enough to make Ayla go into hiding and fear for her life?" Simone took a bite out of a pear tart and gave Eve a big head nod in approval.

"Yeah, and kill anyone who saw what happened or knew what he did. Like maybe . . ." Autumn paused for a moment. "Their neighbor." She looked over at Simone to see if her reasoning made sense.

"I could see it. The wrong place at the wrong time during a lunar eclipse. The moon'll bring out the shadow side of anyone." Simone took another bite of the tart as Cornelia Lachlan's voice rose across the table.

"What have you all heard about these strange lights in the mountain region?" She folded her hands on the table and looked between Jo and Penny. "I for one am concerned after all the happenings over the past several months. I don't want any more . . ."—she chose her words carefully, knowing there were non-magical townsfolk at the table—"mishaps, and the origin of these lights worries me a great deal."

"Oh, Cornelia," Mrs. Pendleton replied. "I wouldn't worry, love. The lights don't seem to have anything to do with our daily life. I would chalk them up to random sundogs in the sky. You know we've had odd days with cold temperatures lately. It's probably just people seeing flashes when the sun reflects the ice."

Mrs. Pendleton directed her eyes to the other end of the table and found Autumn eyeing her strangely. Remembering the day she and Simone saw the flash in the trees between their cottage and Mrs. Pendleton's house, Autumn sensed Mrs. Pendleton concealing something. Yet, her insight couldn't discern what it was yet.

Breaking the gaze with Autumn, Mrs. Pendleton quickly grabbed a tray from the center of the table and raised it to change focus. "Scone, anyone?"

CHAPTER 14

Autumn slammed the door on the passenger side of Simone's SUV and headed toward the torch lights planted throughout the darkening Blake County fairgrounds that night. Simone, Lainy, and Eve followed beside her as they all grew mesmerized by the scene. A giant bonfire blazed in the center of the fair while costumed people dressed as majestic stags with giant antlers danced around the fire. The festival marked the new year of the stag, a representation of grace, power, and wisdom. It portended to be a time of regeneration for the mountain region.

"This is incredible!" Eve's jaw dropped open as she scanned the festival grounds.

Simone nodded. "Yeah, they do it up pretty big every year. Have you not come before?"

Eve shook her head. "No, my family's usually really busy at the Forest Brew with all the lunar new year orders. But this year my mom knew the coven needed me, so she's covering and doing some of the extra baking."

Autumn tilted her head toward Eve. "That was nice of her because we really need you, Eve. You're a huge part of this coven."

Eve pressed her hands down into the patch pockets of her toggle coat and twisted from side to side a bit with contentment. She had never felt like such a part of something before joining the Hollow's Glenn coven with the girls.

"All right, we better get to it," Autumn suggested. "We need to find out more about Delia Hall's whereabouts and any potential clues for where Ayla may be. We've already had one person in Hollow's Glenn say that they saw her, so maybe someone here knows more."

"Right. I say we wander toward that giant publisher's booth over there first." Lainy pointed to the side where a tall display promoted the latest mystical books on oracles and spirit animals. "Didn't you say Delia wanted to get Ayla's book deal?"

"That's right," Autumn confirmed as she started walking in that direction with the girls following. "I guess this publishing house is a big deal, and it could make someone's business skyrocket. Let's see what we can find out."

Autumn made her way up to the large khaki tent with people lounging around as they chatted on large rugs and meditation pillows on the ground. Stacks of books surrounded them on side tables and crates, while lantern lights hung above to light the space with cozy warmth. Catching the eye of a middle-aged woman dressed in palazzo pants and a cropped coat, Autumn took a few steps toward her.

"Excuse me, do you work for the publisher?" Autumn pointed to the books stacked beside the woman.

"Yes, we're here for a promotional event. Every year our publishing house attends a few events to scope out new talent and find the next major voice in the mystical space." She lifted a book about crystals from the top of a stack. "For instance, one of our most popular authors wrote this book. The world has lauded her use of crystals."

Autumn nodded as Simone joined her. "I see. So, you must look into lots of talented mystics. Do you research them ahead of these events, or do they come to you while you're here?"

"Many times we know who we're interested in ahead of time. This year, we've been looking at a few up-and-coming fortune tellers. Unfortunately, the one I was most curious about seems to be missing this year. We may have to see who pops up, after all." The woman gave the girls a crooked smile and eyed another customer. "Well, please, keep looking and let me know if you need anything else."

Simone raised her eyebrows at her cousin. "Well, we already knew most of that except apparently they haven't seen Ayla here. If that book deal was important to her business, then I'm not sure what would have made her stay away, apart from . . ."

Autumn sighed and finished Simone's thought. "From fearing for her life, being held against her will, or already being dead."

"Yeah, not the most ideal of choices, I'd say." Simone brushed her hand through her dark hair as a loud group of women chatted on the ground beside them.

"Oh, I had the most wonderful time at that retreat center for the eclipse!" a woman about Autumn's age said as she placed crystals on a star-shaped grid on the rug in front of her. "We did yoga, drank loads of matcha, and I even got a reading from that palm reader while I was there!"

Leaning down to tap the woman on the shoulder, Autumn smiled. "Sorry, but did you say you went to a retreat center where there was a palm reader?"

The woman nodded and rose to her knees to speak with Autumn. "Yes, you have to try the place! It's the New Dawn Rejuvenation Center. Have you heard of it?" Shaking her head, Autumn let the woman go on. "Oh, well, their eclipse package was fantastic and all-inclusive. The palm reader who gave us the readings at the retreat center is also here at the booth across the way." The woman pointed straight across the fairgrounds to a prominent booth that read Fortune Teller.

"So, she was there during the eclipse for your retreat?" Simone interjected.

"That's right. She was there for the full three days of the retreat, I think. I had never done a palm reading before, but she got me to relax and ease into the reading. She told me everything I needed to know for the new year. You should check her out." The woman lowered back down on her heels and continued arranging the crystals on the ground with a friend.

"Thanks!" Autumn waved to them before turning away.

"I bet Delia made her feel relaxed and willing to go with the flow." Simone rolled her eyes. "What a con artist! Using these potions to convince people to pay for readings that probably aren't even reliable!"

Autumn pressed the palms of her hands down in the air, trying to signal Simone to calm down. "We don't know how real her gifts really are, just that she's using the potions to enhance them and get people more interested than they would be otherwise."

"Exactly, so she's trouble, and I don't like the energy she's putting out around the mountain region. It gives a tainted feeling to every place she goes." Simone shuddered at the thought.

"I agree, but that doesn't mean she's behind Ayla's disappearance or the neighbor's murder. You heard that woman just now. She saw Delia at the retreat center during the lunar eclipse. That gives her an alibi that I bet the retreat center will most likely confirm. So, that puts us down a suspect and with little clues to go on."

The girls met up with Lainy and Eve at the bonfire in the center of the grounds. Sparks flew high above them, and Lainy darted her eyes back and forth to make them swirl in distinct patterns.

Lainy smirked as she watched her silent handiwork. "Sometimes I just love knowing what I can secretly do."

Eve tucked her chin into her coat collar as she laughed. "Hey! Did you guys find any clues? We saw you talking to some people and didn't want to interfere with the conversation."

"Actually, yes. For one thing, it doesn't sound like the publisher has seen Ayla at all, even though they most likely came to see her specifically. But, the biggest thing we found out was that Delia has an alibi." Autumn watched as a tall stag-costumed dancer strode right up to her, quickly circled her, and moved back toward the other dancers.

"So, Delia didn't do it? That's surprising considering she's got 'evil villain' written all over her." Lainy turned to look back at the large fortune teller booth with Delia sitting inside giving readings. "Just look at all the dark-purple shimmers around that tent. Anyone with a real gift would stay miles away from that place." The three other girls nodded their heads in agreement and then turned back to the bonfire.

"What do you all say? Should we grab some apple fritters and head back to the house?" Autumn lifted her hand toward the fritter stand and beckoned the smell in the girls' direction to make it even more pronounced under their noses.

Simone's legs buckled. "Mmm, you read my mind. There's no point in staying out here and watching these stags dance around when we could eat apple fritters."

After they each grabbed a warm fritter and made their way toward the front of the fairgrounds, the girls stopped by the entrance to admire the lit-up scene one final time.

"It really is beautiful with the fire display and the torches. I think this year is going to be memorable!" Eve licked her fingers and nodded as a few men pushed out of the fair office building where Autumn and Simone had visited a few days prior.

"Gibson's land will make a fine addition to this fairground parcel! We just need his wife, Amelia, to agree to sell. She's a stubborn one." The man turned away from the others to reveal himself as the same one they'd seen storming out of Mr. Doyle's office days ago and suspiciously showing up at the downtown riverfront park.

"We'll get her on board, Commissioner." An unfamiliar man shook the commissioner's hand, and they parted ways.

As soon as the commissioner noticed the girls eyeing him, he shifted to avoid making eye contact and hurried to a car in the lot. Autumn eyed him intently as he rushed away.

Standing alone near the office now, Mr. Doyle spotted Autumn and Simone under the large torch lights of the entrance archway. "Oh, hello again! Autumn, was it?" He drew closer to the girls and pulled out his hand for a shake. "And Simone, right?"

Autumn shook his hand and smiled. "That's right, Mr. Doyle. It's a beautiful celebration! We were just admiring it before we headed out for the evening."

"Yes, it turned out quite extraordinary this year." He turned to Autumn and lowered his voice. "I'm sorry Ayla couldn't be here to see it."

The girls gave him tight-lipped smiles of regret before Autumn piped up again. "Uh, Mr. Doyle?" She placed her hand gently on his back and moved to the side with him. "I couldn't help but overhear the commissioner on his way out. Was he referring to Philip Gibson, by any chance?"

"Oh, yes, Philip Gibson. You know him?" Mr. Doyle made a *tisk* noise. "You no doubt saw the article in the paper recently about his death. Yes, well, it's a tragedy, but he's got some land holdings directly next to the fairgrounds. It might be a good thing all around for his wife to sell and add the property to this piece here. At least, that's what some people want to see happen."

"But you don't?" Autumn looked up at him while something told her there was something he wasn't saying.

He sighed and scanned the fairgrounds. Autumn saw the sense of pride he had in his eyes. "I've worked very hard for the mountain community over the years, Autumn. This fairground holds a special piece of my heart, but . . . change is inevitable, and us old softies eventually see the day when income supersedes nostalgia." He patted her on the arm. "You have a good night now, and let me know if you find out anything more about Ayla." Mr. Doyle walked back into the fairgrounds office as Autumn stood more confused now than ever.

Simone took a few steps toward Autumn and squinted at her. "What did he say?"

Shaking her head, Autumn turned to look out toward the rocky grounds and sparsely filled trees to the left and right of the fairgrounds. "I don't quite know, but Mr. Gibson owned land out here. And someone now wants it for financial gain."

CHAPTER 15

James lifted his water glass above the table where Autumn sat across from him. "To finally sharing a nice meal together."

She raised her glass to meet his and clinked them together. "Cheers." Autumn smiled and took a sip of her water as she looked around the well-appointed restaurant where they sat for a late lunch. "You know, this place is really nice. I can't believe I've never eaten here before."

He chuckled at her. "Well, is it any wonder? Marion Bennett and her husband were never exactly best friends with your family, so why would you frequent their restaurant?"

"I know, but I've actually come to appreciate Marion over the past few months. So, I want to support her husband's business just as she's supporting the preservation committee. And besides, the food tastes great. How's your chicken piccata?" Autumn pointed with her fork to James's dish.

"Yeah, it's good. Have a taste." He pushed his plate closer to the middle of the table so she could reach it. "What about your salmon and creamed spinach?"

Autumn took another bite of her own dish and closed her eyes, nodding. "Mmm, divine. You're gonna have to take me here more often."

"Deal. As long as I can wrap up the riverwalk renovation quickly, then I'll have more time."

"Remind me to thank your dad for giving you an early afternoon off today. This was a pleasant surprise." Autumn wiped her mouth on her napkin and pushed her chair back. "Let me just say hello to Marion before we finish up. I'll be right back."

"Of course. I'll be here devouring every bit of my food while you're gone." He smiled and watched her walk toward the front of the house.

"Marion, the food is amazing!" Autumn wrapped her arm around Marion standing beside the hostess counter.

"Oh, Autumn! You finally made it in! It's good to see you. It's been a while, with the preservation committee's hiatus for the holidays. Are you ready for this new year?" Marion turned to wave at some customers leaving at the front.

"Yeah." Autumn hesitated. "Our new shop collections of paper fortunes and moon hangings have been selling well, so

Simone and I think this year is kicking off right. How about you?" As soon as she finished speaking, she felt her gran's necklace grow warm on her chest. She casually rubbed the spot overtop her thick sweater and knew it was glowing once again.

Autumn glanced over Marion's shoulder to the other side of the dining room to search for what had set off the necklace. She noticed a familiar man in a suit sitting with the bank manager at a table by the window.

Marion continued as Autumn stared into the distance. "You know my husband and I always keep busy with the local businesses. So, this year will be no different. There's always something more to do for the town! But otherwise, we're well and good." Noticing Autumn's distraction behind her, Marion turned. "Is something wrong?"

"No, I just wondered about that man sitting over there. Isn't he a commissioner for the county over?" Autumn tried not to look directly at him.

Marion searched the tables and found the one Autumn meant. "Oh, yes, that's Commissioner Craig. He's become a regular lately. Seems he's got quite the network around the mountain region, and word is he's just getting started."

"Hmm, interesting." Autumn put her arms out to hug Marion one more time. "Well, I just wanted to say hello and thank you for the lovely meal. I'll see you once the preservation meetings start back up for the year."

Marion grew busy again, managing the front desk with the hostess as more prominent faces walked in the door. "Yes, thank you, Autumn." She waved and went on to the next guest, taking their coat and making small talk as they entered the restaurant.

As Autumn walked back to James at the table, she wondered why a county commissioner would have business in Hollow's Glenn, and with the bank manager no less. She sat back down across from James and stared at her plate.

"Well, I don't know what to think of that look. Is everything okay?" He stretched his hand out across the table, searching for hers.

She smiled and met his warm brown eyes before holding his hand. "Mm-hmm, yeah. It's just . . ." She lowered her voice so that only he could hear. "I saw the same county commissioner here who's been out at the fairgrounds and at the downtown park the other night. He's eating with the Hollow's Glenn bank manager now."

"Okay . . . And that's a bad thing?" James stared at her in confusion.

"Maybe. I can't be sure. I felt my locket glowing as I talked with Marion, and then I saw him there." She took another swig of her water and grabbed her coat and bag. "Something's going on, and I can't put my finger on it. It's like all the evidence around Mr. Gibson's death and your aunt's disappearance is right in front of me, but I can't see it."

"Almost like an eclipse. Hiding what's in plain sight." James stood and signed for the check before putting his coat on.

"Exactly . . . An eclipse." She followed him to the door and took a big breath of fresh air once stepping outside. "The evidence is there, but we need to clear out the shadows to see it."

Autumn snuggled up beside James in his tall charcoal pickup truck. She pressed her lips to his and took in the scent of chestnuts and cherry cordial. Feeling the warmth of his energy never got old.

"Thanks for having a late lunch with me. It was nice to just spend time with you even though there's still a lot going on." He smiled and brushed the hair back from Autumn's face.

She sat back on the passenger seat and sighed. "I know what you mean. Now that I'm the four-points witch, it feels like there's always something mysterious happening, and I'm always caught right in the middle of it. I miss spending normal days in the shop, taking quiet walks in my sanctuary forest near the cottage, and just spending time with the people I really care about." Her eyes formed tears as she spoke, and she stared out the side window, trying to bat them away.

"Hey." He put his arm around her and pulled her close. "You're doing a great job leading the founding families and keeping the energy in balance. And you have every right to take time for yourself in between these messes you've been cleaning up." He squeezed her tighter in his arms. "God, you could have been killed just a few months ago, and we all just need to be thankful that you're here." He pulled away to look her in the eyes. "I know I am."

"Me, too." Autumn smiled at him, shaking off the tears. "Okay, where to next?"

"Actually, I need a couple things from the hardware store for the job site tomorrow. Do you wanna go with me or should I drop you off first?" He took the truck out of park and waited for her to reply.

"I'll go with you. There's no need to go out of your way since we're close to the store now." She fiddled with the radio and found some Celtic folk music playing.

James turned the corner and headed for the hardware store. The sun had just gone beyond the mountains, and he squinted at the silhouettes in front of him. As he pulled up along the street in front of the store, James pointed as he held the steering wheel.

"Isn't that . . . Brodie?" James squinted harder as he pulled the truck into the lot and stayed to the far side.

"Your uncle? Ayla's husband?" Autumn craned her neck to scan the parking lot. "You're right. There he is loading things into his truck."

James parked his truck on the side of the hardware store to remain out of sight but still have a view of Brodie's truck.

"What's all that stuff he's loading? Looks like big bags of sand and a bunch of chemical barrels." Autumn turned the radio down and sat on the edge of her seat to get a better look.

"Yeah, it does. Shovels, gravel, chemicals . . . Looks like he's hooking up a trailer, too." James turned his back on the windshield so Brodie wouldn't see him as he walked past to go inside the store.

"What do you think he's up to? Something at Ayla's property?" Autumn stared out the windshield at Brodie's truck in confusion.

When Brodie came back out of the store, he carried a slip of paper in his hands and waved to someone on the far side of the store. A man driving a skid steer waved back and followed him toward his trailer, driving the equipment onto it before walking away.

"He's got a skid steer now." James sat back and thought for a moment. "I'm pretty sure the police let him stay at the house now since they've collected all the evidence from Mr. Gibson's death." He rubbed his hand over his stubble beard. "Brodie's never been one to work the land. He never even cared about that property since it belonged to my family for generations. It always seemed like a bitter topic around him."

"He could be trying to cover something up. Maybe something the police never found?" Autumn tried piecing together whatever she could. "There's so much land out there. It's completely possible that we all missed something."

James sighed. "Yeah, a skid steer, shovels, sand, chemicals . . . You could do a lot of covering up with those. Either for something that's still out there or something you're planning to do."

CHAPTER 16

"Who are you texting?" James glanced over at Autumn as he drove them over to Jo and Penny's house.

"Simone. I'm telling her to get the coven together at Aunt Jo's house right away. We've gotta tell them what we saw and figure out what to do before something bad happens." Autumn's fingers typed furiously on her phone.

James watched the anxiousness building inside her. "Okay, let's take a breath. I want to find Aunt Ayla more than anyone, and there's no way I'd let anything bad happen to her. But, Autumn, we have to be smart about this." James pulled the truck into Jo's driveway and got out with Autumn as she rushed to the front porch.

"Come on! Something tells me we can't delay!" She held the front door open for him as Jo came to meet them.

Jo looked between them and wiped her hands on her apron. "Oh, dear. I had a feeling I'd have a houseful this evening . . . And not for a good reason. What happened?"

"Autumn and I saw my uncle Brodie at the hardware store, and Autumn sensed that something wasn't right. And when she gets an insight about something." He paused and tilted his head at Jo.

"We should listen," Jo finished. "Come in the kitchen, dears. Penny, Sim, and Lainy have arrived already."

A knock came at the front door. "I'm here!" Eve stumbled in with a large jug in her mitten hands. She walked it back to the kitchen where they all gathered and stood the jug up tall on the island. "It's my cinnamon chai tea but iced instead of hot. I thought we could use the caffeine and the bit of luck it gives tonight for whatever we might be doing." She shrugged as she looked around the room at the coven.

Autumn grabbed Eve and kissed her forehead. "Eve, you're a genius! That's perfect for what I'm thinking."

"Uh-oh. Autumn's ideas are churning. Should we all be worried?" Lainy grabbed some glasses and began pouring some of Eve's tea for everyone.

"No, I like this side of her!" Simone grabbed a glass from Lainy and nodded in thanks. "Autumn, your air energy gets amplified when the fire comes out. This four-points thing is really working for you."

"All right, girls. Let's just hear what Autumn and James have to say first." Jo fiddled with the rings on her fingers as she waited with worry. "Go ahead, dear."

"Right, well, first things first. I saw that county commissioner again at the Bennetts' restaurant having dinner with the bank manager. Something is definitely going on that seems to be a bit underhanded, but I haven't quite figured that out yet." Autumn took a sip of the tea and closed her eyes. "Oh, Eve, this is so good!"

James smiled and took over for Autumn. "But that wasn't the only or the strangest thing we saw tonight."

"No?" Penny questioned. "What else happened that's gotten you all stirred up?"

"Brodie." James looked at Aunt Jo to share in her concern. "My uncle, Ayla's husband, who she kicked out a while ago, is definitely back, just as Eve heard. This evening Autumn and I saw him buying supplies at the hardware store. Chemicals, shovels, sand, a skid steer. Things that wouldn't be necessary for anything other than digging around or—"

"Covering things up," Simone interjected. "Wow, that's subtle. Buying everything you need to get rid of a body and hide it right in front of the whole town." She paused and felt a twinge of guilt for saying that out loud. "Sorry, James. That was insensitive with your aunt going missing."

He shook his head at her. "No, it's okay. You're just stating the obvious, and I appreciate that about you."

"Anyway, if Ayla is out there somewhere and he's planning to do something, then this is our chance to deter him. Either that or figure out what he's really hiding." Autumn put her iced tea down on the island.

"How do we do that?" Eve shrugged and looked around the room. "We don't want him to know we're onto him."

"Yes, and I don't want anything to happen to you girls." Penny crossed her arms as she rubbed her hands over them. "We have no idea what this man is capable of, and I don't want another missing person or worse."

Autumn shared a glance with Simone, silently exchanging thoughts with her before speaking up with confidence. "That's exactly why it's time for a stakeout."

Autumn opened the hatchback of Simone's SUV and let a hint of light onto the dark road past the Ross property where the car sat. She routed around before finding a small wicker basket of supplies and pulling out the ancestral feather of a boreal mountain owl that her mother had kept for her over many years. With it, she knew that wisdom once hidden would come to light. As she tucked it gently into the inside pocket of her wool coat, she heard a meow coming from underneath a flannel blanket.

A furry head popped out from under the flannel and looked up at Autumn with sweet but mischievous eyes. "You just love to go wherever there's trouble, don't you?" She snatched the cat into her arms. "All right, you can come with us, but stay close and be quiet."

Eve came around to the back of the SUV beside her. "Everything okay?"

Autumn nodded. "Yeah, Tav just decided to tag along tonight." She gave him a head scratch, and Eve did the same. "I can't say I'm mad, though. He's gotten me out of more sticky situations than I'd like to admit. So, if he's here, then that means we better be on our toes and keep him close."

Eve quietly shut the trunk door and walked with Autumn to meet Simone and Lainy in the dark woods beside Ayla's property. The moon waned to a quarter of its size now, and it shone down on the trees, casting strange shadows on the rocky ground below.

"I see his truck over at the house," Simone whispered. "The lights are on inside, but I heard him rummaging around on the back porch."

"We should probably stick to the woods and keep our distance," Lainy suggested.

"Yeah, good call." Autumn nodded as she stepped as quietly as possible through the rocky terrain. Stopping at a large log pile mounded a few feet high, she dropped Tavish to the ground and scanned the trees. They stood within the tree line but far enough away from the house as not to be seen. "How about we put that cloaking spell we've been practicing to use?"

Eve bounced up and down on her tiptoes. "Yes!" she excitedly whispered. "Simone, come stand over here beside me. This is the perfect spot for us to mark the boundaries from."

Autumn smiled and turned to Lainy. "Keep watch for us, will you? There's still a chance someone could see or hear us until I get the spell done."

Lainy nodded. "I'm on it. You just do the spell, and I'll keep a lookout."

Tavish kept close to Autumn's side as she moved nearer to Eve and Simone a few paces into the woods. The two girls stood back-to-back, lifting their right palms in the air to prepare for Autumn's spell.

"Ready when you are, Autumn." Eve gave her a head nod to confirm.

Autumn took in a deep breath and exhaled as the surrounding winds shifted. Her hair swirled as she rubbed her hands together, feeling the anger within her that someone had brought more death and fear into Hollow's Glenn. With the thought, a spark formed in her hands, and she revealed a large flame in her left palm.

Holding it in front of her, Autumn spoke the words for the cloaking spell as she had done in practice. "Elements of earth, air, fire, and water, protect us from outside eyes and ears.

Conceal us with the energy of a thick forest, mounted to the sky."

As she spoke the words, Eve and Simone moved their hands in large clockwise circles to cast the cloaking boundaries.

Autumn opened her mouth to continue the spell as Lainy shouted, "He's coming! Get down!"

The back porch light flickered on, and the door slammed as the large man in a thick flannel jacket stomped down the porch steps with a stack of papers in one hand and a bottle in the other. Autumn snuffed her flaming hands out by quickly blowing a burst of air into them. She crouched down next to Lainy behind the log pile, and the girls watched as Brodie threw the papers down on a small pile of wood in the center of the property.

He shook his bottle over the top of it and pulled out a box from his jacket pocket. Striking a match, he threw it onto the pile and stepped back, watching it burn. Brodie laughed as he took another swig of his drink, emptying the bottle before throwing it to the ground. He stumbled over a few rocks and turned his foot over to see some pebbles caught in the treads of his boots.

Lainy leaned over to whisper in Autumn's ear. "He's a mess. No wonder Ayla finally got rid of him."

Brodie found a stick and picked at the pebbles on the bottoms of his boots before tossing it aside and making his way over to his truck parked on the side of the house.

The girls pushed back from the edge of the log pile as Brodie moved around the house. Autumn turned to face Eve and Simone. "I need to finish the spell. Just envision the boundary in your mind."

As Brodie pulled the latch open on his truck bed, he pulled out a shovel and walked over to the edge of the tree line close to the girls. He jammed the shovel blade into the ground and scooped a hole in the hard rock.

Autumn whispered under her breath, "We draw a boundary around us four. By the—" She leaned slightly forward, and a stick cracked beneath her knee.

Brodie stopped shoveling at the sound and eyed the tree line suspiciously. "Who's there?" He swallowed hard and took a few steps to the side to get another perspective of the trees.

Tavish sat up on his hind legs and pawed at Autumn's coat. She shook her head at the cat, not wanting him to attract attention, but he continued pawing at the left side of her wool jacket. Autumn stopped for a minute and realized she had placed the owl feather inside her coat pocket.

She carefully removed the feather and visualized a night owl swooping down from the trees. "Swift owl, hear my call." Autumn summoned the bird under her breath, and in an instant a sound carried from high above the trees.

Looking up over the property, Brodie watched as an owl with outstretched wings circled above the small fire.

"What the?" He turned in circles, watching the owl dive toward him and then back up into the sky.

"Lainy, the fire." Autumn dipped her chin toward the fire Brodie had made.

Nodding with understanding, Lainy concentrated her energy on the fire in front of him and lifted her palms in front of her. With one large swoop of her hand, the flames rose high above, sending Brodie stumbling back onto the ground.

Autumn quickly finished the cloaking spell as he fell. "We draw a boundary around us four, and with the power of three, so shall it be."

Eve and Simone stood and circled their arms around three times to cast the boundary as Brodie dragged himself to his feet behind a roaring fire.

The girls stood firmly at their position in the trees, waiting to see if the spell worked. Brodie scanned the trees once again as the girls stood directly in front of him now, but he saw and heard nothing.

Simone tugged at Autumn's sleeve. "Come on, cuz. It's time to go."

The girls turned and started slowly walking out of the woods as Brodie stood confused by the fire. Tavish paused and perked up his ears in the center of the trees, sensing something to come.

A flash of light burst through the forest from the far end of the trees. Autumn turned, covering her eyes with her hand as the light dissipated to darkness again.

"That was it, wasn't it?" Eve took a few hurried steps out into the forest past the girls. "That was the mysterious mountain light!"

"Eve, wait! We need to get out of here," Lainy called, as their voices remained concealed by the cloaking spell.

"Ayla?" Brodie's voice echoed behind them near the roaring fire.

The girls stopped abruptly and turned to see a woman in a long A-line dress and boots casually strolling out of the darkness on the far side of the property. Strands of hair blew free of her loose braid, and dark-purple shimmers trailed behind her.

"Ayla, it is you! I . . . I'm back, my darling girl," he stammered as he watched her appear in the light of the fire and the moon.

She stood eyeing him for a moment and then looked up at the quarter moon. Drawing her hand up to the sky as if pulling at a piece of the moon, she pinched her fingers together and let them open toward him. Small purple shimmers floated in his direction and swirled around his face.

"If I am your darling . . . then you are my minion."

Jo's Waxing Moon Confidence Bath

As the moon brightens, take some time to draw a hot bath. Add the following ingredients to the water:

5-10 orange slices (dried or fresh)

2 Tbsp chamomile or yellow rose flowers

3-5 drops rosemary essential oil

Light three yellow candles and place in a safe position beside the bath. As you immerse yourself into the water, repeat the following words three times:

I embrace the fire to match the water.

Now, close your eyes as you feel the hot water on your skin and focus on your inner strength. Feel the heat raising your confidence along with the temperature of your body. Take a deep breathe and feel strong and connected to your body and spirit.

CHAPTER 17

E ve pushed two mugs of peppermint hot chocolate across the bar of the Forest Brew to Autumn and Simone. Taking a sip, Autumn licked the whipped cream from her top lip and closed her eyes.

"I love having a friend who knows her way around the kitchen." Autumn opened her eyes again to see Eve in front of her with a giant grin.

"Yeah, tell me about it." Simone leaned over and nudged Autumn's shoulder from the next bar stool over. "Can we just hire her to make all our meals?"

Eve giggled as she wiped down the counter. "I'm really glad you like everything! I have been working hard on my new . . . recipes." She winked before continuing her cleaning. "Anyway, let me put your order in for those cheese melts and get those started." She turned away from the girls and looked up toward the register. As soon as she saw the familiar face placing an order, she gasped and stumbled back, almost spilling the coffeepot on the back counter.

Autumn stood abruptly. "Eve, are you okay?"

Eve gathered herself together again. "I'm fine. Just gonna place your order over here." She motioned with her pointer finger toward the counter while tilting her head in that direction. "Yep, just placing that order."

Simone and Autumn followed Eve's obvious pointing to find Brodie Aitken standing at the counter, giving his order to Mrs. Newbury. She looked to be making small talk with the man as Eve stood beside her mother and listened quietly.

Simone leaned over to whisper in Autumn's ear. "Well, isn't he a man about town now?" She took a long swig of her hot chocolate and perked up again. "He doesn't know who we are, right?"

"I don't think so," Autumn said, shaking her head. "The cloaking spell seemed to work last night." Taking a sip of her own drink, she felt a pang of warmth around her neck. She bent over the counter, placing the mug down as if the heat had burned her tongue, when really the intense warmth of the locket had startled her.

"Are you okay?" Simone squinted her eyes at her cousin's sudden jerkiness.

"Mm-hmm, yeah. It's the locket. It's practically burning against my skin." Autumn eyed Brodie before moving her gaze behind him and out the front window of the Forest Brew.

Out on the street, two women, Delia Hall and Ayla Ross, talked. They stood close to one another as if familiar with each other. Yet just yesterday, Ayla was missing and Delia had stolen her festival booth and her potential book deal.

Autumn nudged Simone and turned toward the window. They watched as Delia gently patted Ayla's arm and nodded. The two of them looked like they had been secret friends for years. As Delia was about to leave, a man in a tailored wool coat and dark scarf turned the corner and bumped into them. Hesitating when he saw their faces, he took a step back and turned abruptly, looking at the ground before heading in the other direction.

As the man crossed at the streetlight and pulled his scarf down, Autumn stood to get a better look at him. She noticed the familiar stature of a well-dressed man who kept popping up around the region. When he made it across the street, the man showed his face and confirmed himself as County Commissioner Craig.

"Him again." Autumn put her hands on her hips and thought for a moment as the bell chimed at the front door.

"Oh my! It is you!" Mrs. Newbury called as she made her way around the counter to embrace Ayla Ross at the front door.

Simone stood up to get a better view as she pulled her phone out of her back jeans pocket. "I'm texting my mother. She'll let the chief and Sorcha know Ayla's here."

Autumn nodded as they sat back on their stools so as not to cause a distraction. "Good idea. I'm sure they'll all have some questions for her."

As soon as she sat down again, Autumn sensed a hushing sound through the coffee shop. The voices swept through and whispered a message to her in the air.

"Those who wear masks conceal the light," the whispers repeated once more as she eyed Ayla, who was now sitting down across from Brodie in the front window and directing him to sit up straighter.

Eve rushed back to the girls. "I just dialed the police station from the kitchen. Chief Walsh should be over any minute." She noticed Autumn staring off into the distance, and she waved her hand in front of her face. "Autumn, are you okay?" She glanced at Simone, and they shrugged at each other.

"Autumn, what's up?" Simone shook her cousin's arm and lowered her voice. "Is it the locket?"

"Yeah, uh, no." Autumn grabbed her hot chocolate mug and thought for a moment. "The voices . . . Something about people wearing masks." She sighed and brought the mug up to her nose to inhale a deep scent of peppermint for some clarity. "I feel like everyone's hiding something right now. It's hard to tell who's guilty and who's not. And now that I saw Ayla with

Delia out on the street . . . it's hard to believe that even she isn't up to something."

Just as she finished her thought, Autumn noticed Ian and Ben Walsh walking through the front door casually as ever. No one would have imagined they'd been looking for a suspected murderer for days, along with the then-missing woman who had just wandered in for some coffee.

The chief searched the coffee shop, and Mrs. Newbury pointed him to the window table. He tipped his hat at her and walked with Ben over to Ayla and Brodie's table.

"Morning, Brodie." Chief Walsh eyed him for a moment as Brodie grunted at him. "Ayla, you've been missing for some time now. It's good to see you back safely, but we have some questions for you. Would you mind stepping outside with us for a few minutes?"

Ayla smiled innocently at the chief as another chime came from the front door. Sorcha Allan burst in with Josephine right behind her.

Wrapping her hands around her mouth, Sorcha shook her head in disbelief. Tears formed in her eyes, and she scurried over to her sister, wrapping her arms around her as she sobbed.

"Where have you been? I was so scared that . . ." Sorcha turned to see Brodie sitting across the table from her sister. "Brodie, I see you've made yourself comfortable here with Ayla again. Was this your doing? Are you the reason my sister's been missing, and that poor man from across the street . . .?" She choked up again without getting all the words out.

Chief Walsh wrapped his arm around Sorcha and pulled her back toward Josephine. He sighed. "Jo, would you please?"

Jo nodded and immediately took Sorcha over to the back counter to find Autumn and Simone sitting there. They all stared as Ben escorted Ayla outside to a bench where the chief could ask her some questions.

Brodie turned to find the whole coffee shop staring at him with wide eyes. "Don't look at me! She just showed up!" He let out a deep sigh and went back to his coffee, flipping up the collar of his jacket and burying his head into it.

"Girls, what's going on?" Josephine rubbed Sorcha's shoulders as she talked.

"Ayla appeared last night, Mom." Simone kept her voice quiet and low. "When we were out on their property, another flash of light appeared, and then there she was."

"Yeah, she just appeared out of the darkness." Chills rose up Autumn's spine as she said the words. She glanced over at Sorcha on the end and reached a hand out toward hers. "We'll figure this out, Mrs. Allan, but at least she's safe."

"Well, if it isn't some of the most fascinating people in Hollow's Glenn," a woman's voice chimed in from behind Autumn.

"Anabeth…" Simone wondered how she always popped up just as they were discussing important details to be kept under wraps. "Grabbing some lunch before a busy day of reporting? Who's this?" Simone lifted her chin toward the unsuspecting guy wearing a denim collared shirt and loose tie beside her. He appeared a bit disheveled, but Simone saw his canary-yellow aura mixed with hints of turquoise blue. There was definitely something intellectual and quietly understanding about him.

"Oh, this is Finn." Anabeth pointed her thumb in his direction. "He's new to *The Glenn Herald*, so I'm showing him the ropes. They wanted him to see the major stories as they unfold. Seems he'll be shadowing me on the front lines of that fracking story for a while."

He waved his hand through the air at them. "Hi." With a tight-lipped smile, he brought his hands back together as he clasped a notebook and pen.

Autumn watched as a line of golden shimmers traced through the air after his hand and then circled the pen clasped within his fingers. "Finn . . . are you originally from Hollow's Glenn?"

Finn wrapped his hands behind his back, trying to hide anything he didn't want seen. "Uh, no, but my aunt and uncle live here. The Carmichaels."

Jo gasped and placed her hand over her chest. "Oh, you're Rose's nephew! Well, any family of the Carmichaels is always welcome here. I'm Josephine MacKinnon, and this is my daughter, Simone, and my niece, Autumn. You just let any of us know if you need help settling in. Rose knows where to find us." Jo moved her gaze down to Sorcha sobbing again on the stool beside where she stood. "Goodness, you've caught us at a terrible time. You'll have to excuse us while we attend to some serious matters." Jo helped Sorcha off the stool and toward the front door to meet up with Chief Walsh, Ben, and Ayla.

Autumn watched as they spoke before Ayla came inside again to sit with Brodie. Ayla seemed to be pleased with herself as she completely ignored her sister's distress before getting back to her lunch.

"Anyway, Autumn?" Anabeth tapped Autumn's shoulder. "I see Ayla Ross is back in town after the mysterious disappearance. Have you heard anything more about the neighbor's death? I know they've called it a murder, but no evidence was released to that effect."

"Right, uh . . ." Autumn watched Anabeth stare at her, waiting, as a thought came to her. "Actually, you know what, Anabeth? You mentioned a major story about fracking. Didn't you say before that there's some kind of illegal fracking ring in the mountain region?"

Anabeth's eyebrows rose. "Yes, what have you heard? Is it something we can discuss here?" She slid onto the stool that Sorcha left empty just as Eve popped out of the kitchen with the girls' sandwiches.

"Two cheese melts with spinach salads." Eve placed them down in front of Autumn and Simone and scanned the others at the counter. "Oh, sorry. I didn't realize you were all here. Would you like to order?"

"Hold on a second, Eve. Anabeth was just sharing some information about illegal fracking in the region. Anabeth, you need a lot of land for fracking, don't you?" Autumn eyed Eve and Simone before returning her gaze to Anabeth.

"Yeah, that's right." Anabeth pointed to the broccoli and cheese soup on the menu and held up two fingers to Eve. "To go, please." Eve nodded to her and jotted it down as she listened to Anabeth continue. "You need a ton of rocky shale or hard clay with fossil fuel below it. It's a pretty big job to get all those resources from the land, so it requires a significant amount of digging and equipment."

"Digging, uh?" Autumn took a bite of her sandwich and pulled the extra stringy cheese away from her mouth.

"Oh, yeah. First, there's lots of testing, grading of the land, prepping it for drilling . . . All kinds of stuff. It's a big deal, and right now it's illegal in the region." Anabeth turned toward Finn and lowered her voice. "But what did we find out?"

Finn stood up straighter as if he was called up to the blackboard in class. He brushed his brown hair to the side of his forehead and cleared his throat. "Apparently there's some corruption in the next county over. Some of the elected officials seem to turn a blind eye to what looks like significant fracking arrangements."

"Really?" Simone stabbed at a sliced pear in her spinach salad. "I wonder if that has anything to do with a particular commissioner Autumn's seen networking around town lately."

Anabeth perked up at Simone's comment. "Oh, really? Anyone I might know?"

Autumn stared at her plate and poked at her food. "Craig, I believe. He seems to be suspiciously popular with the bank manager here in town."

"Interesting." Anabeth dipped her chin to signal Finn to write that down. "What else are you thinking?"

Autumn looked directly at Anabeth and sighed. "That this could be the reason for a lot of property discussions about town. Not to mention that a substantial amount of rocky land sounds a lot like Ayla Ross's property, and her recently returning husband just happens to have a lot of grading equipment on hand."

CHAPTER 18

Simone put her phone down beside the computer at Parchment and Pine and stood up from her stool. "Mom called. She and Penny are bringing Sorcha and Ayla over here for tea this afternoon. Apparently they think this is a good place to get to the bottom of where she's been."

"Okay . . . This should be interesting." Autumn stood on a stepladder, hanging a few more of their new moon phase decorations to restock for the lunar new year week. "Are you putting the teakettle on, then?"

"Yep, I'll be in the back," Simone shouted as she walked to the back room.

Tavish wandered around the shop and made his way to the front window. He jumped onto the display and peered out at Main Street, watching the people pass. Seeing the familiar ladies wander toward the door, the cat craned his neck around the curtains. He jumped down and met Aunt Jo as she came in brushing her wool cape off with her gloved hands.

Circling her feet, Tavish purred. "Well, hello to you, too." Jo smiled and gave him a rub.

He took a few steps toward the doorway after Penny and Sorcha stumbled inside, and then blocked the way in front of Ayla. The cat stood firmly in place and hissed at her, not allowing her to enter with the rest of them.

Autumn came down from her stepladder and scooped up the cat just as the locket underneath her sweater warmed. Standing up with hesitation, Autumn stared at Ayla with suspicion. "Ayla, I'm so sorry. Come inside, please." Autumn looked down at the cat, wondering what he was thinking, and then dropped him onto the floor in the center of the shop. "Let's go into the hearth room. Simone is coming with the tea."

"That sounds divine." Ayla smiled while keeping a close eye on Tavish.

Sorcha and Ayla took the wingback chairs in the hearth room, and Jo pulled up the ottoman beside Sorcha. Penny found a spot at the base of the fireplace and leaned over to help Autumn and Simone as they laid the tea. Pulling a familiar kraft paper bag out of her satchel, Penny opened it to reveal six tea bags inside. The almond and geranium leaf aromas of Gran's honesty tea came wafting through the air.

Autumn exchanged a glance with her mother and smiled knowingly. This was Penny and Jo's way of getting to the heart of what was going on.

"This looks lovely, girls. Thank you." Penny smiled and tried to keep the air light.

"Ayla, I don't know if you remember me, but I'm Autumn. I've been spending a lot of time with your nephew, James, recently. He's mentioned fond memories of you and of being on the Ross property that you own."

Sorcha watched her sister carefully as Ayla took a teacup and swirled it gently in her hand. "James always loved spending time there. You remember, Ayla?"

Her sister nodded before taking a sip of tea. "Right, family memories are so very important." Her vague response made Sorcha almost wince with disappointment at the lack of acknowledgement.

Sighing as she took a cup of tea from Penny, Sorcha let out her frustration. "Honestly, Ayla. I don't understand what's gotten into you. First, you disappear for days on end and miss our visit. Then, you give up your place at the Lunar Fest, and now you're back with Brodie! I don't even see you wearing the crescent moon necklace you never take off. What's gotten into you?"

Jo scooted closer to Sorcha and patted her hand. "Now, dear, let's try to be patient with Ayla. I sense there's so much going on inside of her."

"Thank you, Josephine." Ayla put her tea down and leaned back in the wingback chair, resting her hands on the arms as if unconcerned with the line of questioning. "I have quite a bit affecting my energy state, and I've been thinking for quite some time about making a few adjustments."

"So you let your best business season go by the wayside and took back the man who's been treating you poorly for decades?" Sorcha's hand shook with anger as she lifted her teacup to her mouth.

"If he stays, I'll make use of him. And if he goes, it will be no matter. My travels are my main focus now. I would have continued wandering as I have been these past few days had it not been for some . . . Unfinished business that needed tending to here." Ayla rolled her eyes before peering through the archway into the rest of the shop. A journal standing upright on a center table caught her eye. She wandered over to it and held it up for Autumn to see. "Is it the ancestral tree?"

With Ayla's words, Penny immediately locked eyes with Jo. They exchanged a thought and returned to Ayla.

Autumn squinted at her. "It's a hawthorn tree. Do you know it?"

"I think I do, yes. I'll take it." Ayla moved to the back counter as Autumn turned to question the rest of them in the hearth room. Penny nodded at Autumn to appease Ayla as Sorcha got up and followed.

"Since when are you interested in traveling and leaving right when we had a visit planned? I was worried sick! And why are you walking out on our tea?" Sorcha stood beside her sister now as she handed Autumn some money at the counter. "Ayla, talk to me!"

Ayla turned and let out a deep breath. "Sorcha, this has become exhausting. Once I decide, I'll let you know when I plan to go again, but I have no intention of staying very long." She turned toward Autumn, scanning her energy for a moment. Lifting the journal, she smiled. "Thank you for the tea, the journal, and . . . the familiar energy."

Heading toward the front door, Ayla walked past Tavish at his perch in the front window. The cat picked himself up at her approach and hissed once again as she walked out the door.

"Well, I never!" Sorcha put her hands on her hips and went to the front window to watch her sister walk away.

"Sorcha, dear, never mind your frustration. Tell us what you're sensing." Jo clasped her hands together as she walked through the shop with her long, flowing green velvet skirt brushing the floor.

Sorcha sighed and sat down beside Tavish on the broad windowsill. "Emptiness, mistrust, apathy . . . All things that I would never associate with my sister. Her energy is gone. It's just completely absent."

"Yes, and I felt a dark cloud hovering within her. One that I've never experienced around Ayla before." Jo crossed her arms over her chest. She looked over at Penelope now behind her. "I don't know if the honesty tea really worked on her, but I believe it gave us a glimpse under the surface."

"Yeah, and who we found there," Simone interjected, winding her arm through her mother's, "doesn't seem to be the person we were looking for."

CHAPTER 19

The coven stood in a circle around a small bonfire in the sanctuary woods beside Gran's cottage. Lainy moved her right palm up and down to direct the flames as her left stayed steady and high.

"Eve, your turn first," Autumn suggested, with Tavish standing guard directly beside her. "Use the earth to snuff out the flames."

Eve nodded from her position on the north end of the bonfire. She lowered herself to the ground and pressed her hands firmly into the earth, whispering, "Earth below me, snuff out the flames. As I say it, so shall it be." Finishing her intention, she flung her hands out in front of her with a huge trail of dirt and golden shimmers. The flecks of dirt splattered onto the edges of the flames, and the strength of the bonfire dissipated.

"Nice! That was pretty good for a few specks of dirt." Simone smirked at her from her point at the west.

"Lainy, keep concentrating and lifting the flames. See if you can fight our spells." Autumn directed the group as she stood in the position of air at the east, even though she knew she wouldn't be able to lead the coven plus stand in place of the air element much longer. They were going to need another air witch for the coven to level up. "Sim, you're next." Autumn nodded to her cousin from across the flames. "Work your water magic."

Simone lifted a stockpot-sized cauldron full of water that she had left outside for collecting rain and snow water. She moved it directly between her and the fire before widening her stance in her black ankle boots. Moving her hands in a clockwise direction and then switching to counterclockwise, she mimicked the rhythm of water. "Extinguish the flames, cool the heat. With my movement, the spell shall be complete."

She rocked from side to side on her toes as she continued moving her hands in a circular motion. The water sloshed in the cauldron with each motion she created. When she felt ready, Simone flung her hands out in front of her, and the entire contents of the cauldron created a tidal wave onto the bonfire.

Lainy wrestled to keep the flames at their original height, but the water suppressed the central section of the fire. Lainy sighed and dropped her arms. "Man, you guys are getting much stronger. I'm glad I'm on your team."

"Yeah, the most awesome elemental magic team that these parts have seen in a century." Eve rose from the ground and put her hands on her hips. "I'm pretty proud of us."

Just as Eve let out the words, a flash of light sparked brightly across the sky. Tavish craned his neck around abruptly and trotted down the path toward the cottage.

"Tavish, wait!" Autumn hurried after him. "Come on," she called back to the others. "It's the same light that Simone and I saw the other day. I wanna see if Jo and Mom were right."

Simone sighed, racing ahead. "Autumn, wait! If it is some weird fae light, then you're not going alone."

Lainy and Eve looked at each other and nodded. With a quick wave of her hand, Lainy extinguished what remained of the bonfire, and the two of them ran to catch up with Autumn and Simone.

"Don't meet the fae without me!" Eve shouted. "I can't believe I'm actually saying that," she panted at Lainy as they made it to the edge of the woods.

Autumn and Simone stood on the opposite side of Gran's cottage with Tavish at their feet. Autumn took a few steps closer to the woods between Hawthorn Cottage and Mrs. Pendleton's house next door.

"There they are," Autumn whispered back to Simone. "The wisps are beckoning me into the trees." She took a few more steps forward with Tavish as they both stared in awe of the tiny sapphire lights appearing on the woods floor. The cat ran up and pounced on one of them but couldn't catch it before it jumped further along.

"I don't see them, but I can feel the energy." Simone squinted at the forest. "To me . . . it's more purple than sapphire blue. Like an ethereal energy."

"What's Autumn see?" Lainy leaned in beside Simone as she and Eve walked up next to her.

"Wisps, I guess. I'm not sure, exactly, but I sense that they're there." Simone took a few steps forward to meet up with Autumn and Tavish.

Eve pointed into the forest and ran up to the edge with excitement. "I see one! It was a little blue light!" She turned to face the rest of them and asked, "Can we go in?"

Sticks cracking beyond the tree line made Eve jump back into line with the others. Autumn watched as a figure emerged from within the small forest. Mrs. Pendleton stood in front of them in her tall rain boots and barn jacket, surrounded by purple shimmers and tiny sapphire wisps.

Smiling and looking directly at Autumn, Mrs. Pendleton stretched out her hand. "I've been expecting you. Come."

Autumn turned to find Simone with her jaw dropped open in disbelief. *Mrs. Pendleton*, Simone mouthed without actually speaking.

Tilting her head down to signal that she intended to follow, Autumn took a few steps into the woods along with Tavish.

The cat trotted up to Mrs. Pendleton and swatted at a few of the wisps while trying to keep up.

"You must have questions." Mrs. Pendleton led them further into the trees until they stopped at a small mushroom circle at the base of the hawthorn tree.

Autumn gazed up at the majestic tree that she remembered being led to many years ago. "The hawthorn."

"You know it." Mrs. Pendleton nodded, pleased with the wisdom Autumn had already shared. "I knew once your gifts opened up to you it would be only a matter of time before the portals activated as well."

"So this is a portal?" Autumn walked up to the tree and placed a hand on it. She sensed the powerful energy flowing within it and knew immediately that it connected to her somehow. "Does it open to the fae world?"

"Mmmm . . . In a way, yes. When the energy activates and something calls to those on the other side, then it opens." Mrs. Pendleton ran her hand along the trunk of the tree as she walked around it.

"Are you saying Autumn activated the portal?" Eve questioned as she watched the wisps continue dancing in the mushroom circle.

"Oh, the eclipse activated the energy. The moon holds a great deal of water energy connected to dreamwork, emotion, and worlds beyond what we see. It primed the doorway to be opened. But the call . . . that is the other matter. Someone who can match the vibration to that on the other side must put out the call. You see, you must have both: the doorway activation and the vibrational call. Usually, for this hawthorn tree"—Mrs. Pendleton sat on a large log beside the mushroom circle—"I maintain the vibration."

Simone stared at Mrs. Pendleton's aura, watching the purple shimmers extend beyond her body into a larger aura. "You're fae."

"Yes, dear." Mrs. Pendleton smiled warmly. "Just like my great niece, Autumn."

Tavish jumped up onto Mrs. Pendleton's lap and rubbed his head along her sleeve as if realizing he had found another long-lost relative to claim for himself.

"Oh, wow! This is huge!" Eve braced her cheeks in her hands and bobbed up and down.

Autumn sat beside Mrs. Pendleton on the log, staring at the ground in confusion. "But, Mrs. Pendleton—"

Mrs. Pendleton put a hand on Autumn's coat sleeve and shook her head. "Please, call me Freya. I'm your great aunt Freya."

"Okay, Freya. You've been here for as long as I can remember, and I've never seen any kind of fae energy around you." Autumn moved her hand around to point to the obvious purple shimmers and wisps surrounding Mrs. Pendleton.

"Your grandmother knew. I suspect she found out many years ago when I bought the house after you were born. I think she kept you close to me so that I would know you as best as I could, and you, me. But, it remained important for my identity to stay hidden until the time was right. Your father wanted me to watch over you but not intervene." Freya searched Autumn's eyes for any hint of awareness of her father or who she really was.

"My mother said his name was Laith," Autumn said as a wisp landed softly on the back of her hand before disappearing.

Freya smiled and nodded. "That's right. She's still connected to him, you know, as are you. Your mother always had the strength of the earth within her, and the fae connect with that energetic vibration very strongly, even across worlds. Your parents connected through the vibration of the dreamscape. That may be something you did not know of your mother's gifts. It was only because of unfortunate events that they parted. And yet, through their connection, he felt your presence and requested that I be here when you claimed your birthright."

Autumn bent down to the ground to get a closer view of the mushroom circle. "What do you mean, my birthright?"

Mrs. Pendleton tilted her head at Autumn. "Oh, sweet girl. Your fae grandmother, my older sister, is Mabel. She ruled over the fae of the light for centuries. And while you are a halfling who has become a powerful witch, you are also the heir to another land."

CHAPTER 20

Simone parked her SUV in front of the town bank and glanced over at her cousin in the passenger seat, wondering if she was going to faint again.

"Are you sure you're okay? Our moms haven't done the new cloaking spell on the town bell yet, and I'm worried we're too close to it. I don't want you keeling over on me again." Simone stared at her cousin and flipped the collar up on her quilted coat.

"Sim, I'm okay. I'll tell you if I feel anything strange again, but honestly, I don't know why you're making me drive over here instead of just walking down Main Street. I'm fine." Autumn grabbed her backpack and pulled the car door open as Simone did the same.

"You just fainted on me and Eve the other day when we were only a block away. Don't tell me you're fine, because I can feel your energy. I know you're worried, so let me be a good cousin and keep you away from that bell, okay?" Simone locked arms with Autumn and gave her the eye.

"All right, fine. Maybe I am a little worried that I can't go where I please in town without feeling really drained, but we have to find out what's going on with the county commissioner. I know Sarah can help us." Autumn pointed to the bank directly in front of them and lifted her chin in that direction.

"I just wish you wouldn't be so stubborn about needing to do everything yourself. We have an entire coven now, remember? Any of us could have come over here." Simone opened the door to the bank lobby and let Autumn in first.

Autumn leaned back and whispered, "I think we both know who the stubborn one is here. Besides, Sarah's known me for years, and I think she's fairly comfortable chatting with me." Autumn caught eyes with her friend across the lobby and waved. "There she is. Let's go see what we can find out." The girls walked across the bank floor to meet a tall, slender woman in a cream suit.

Sarah immediately wrapped her arms around Autumn and started into the conversation. "Autumn, it's so good to see you!" She stood back and gasped. "I heard you had an accident up at the lake a little while back. Are you all right?"

"Oh, yeah, I'm fine. Thanks for asking. I'm all taken care of now, so no need to worry." Autumn smiled at her friend and tried to change the subject. "Anyway, you remember my cousin, Simone? We run the shop together."

Nodding as she looked over her shoulder, Sarah escorted the girls over to her desk and motioned for them to take a seat. "Yeah, of course. How are you, Simone?"

"Good, thanks. Long time no see." Simone wasn't one for chitchat and sat shaking her foot back and forth, wishing they'd get to the point.

"Oh, I'm glad you both came in! You know, Dave and I have been so busy with wedding planning that I haven't seen much of anybody lately!" Sarah waved her hand in the air. "Of course, I have been working like crazy, too, what with all the new accounts coming in."

"Are there new businesses setting up in town or something?" Autumn offered a naïve look to appear casual.

Sarah leaned over her desk a bit and lowered her voice. "Actually, it's all the recent development around the mountain region. From what I hear, there are private investors buying up a ton of land to start some kind of resource management company. I think it's a big deal, because we're moving funding around all over the place. Since I oversee the business accounts at the bank, I've been busy setting up new accounts for these companies."

"Interesting . . . I wonder what land will be affected." Autumn tilted her head innocently.

"I couldn't tell you that, but I bet they're going to be bringing in all kinds of equipment soon. I know they applied for a substantial loan as well. Anyway, I'm just going on and on. What did you come in for today?" Sarah glanced between the two of them, waiting with a smile.

"We just had some questions about the Parchment and Pine account. That's all." Simone gave a quick response off the cuff as she leaned her elbow onto the desk. "You know, we love helping people with their events, like weddings!"

"That's right!" Autumn nodded along. "You know we do all sorts of invitations, decorations, and paper goods for events."

Simone twisted her lips to the side and agreed as Sarah stared at them both, confused. "Yeah, and we're interested in expanding our product lines a bit, but we need to make sure that we'd be secure enough in our finances to launch something bigger."

"Oh, I see. Well, I'd be happy to look over the numbers with you both to see if you should finance or if your regular business will sustain you. Should we look now?" Sarah raised an eyebrow and started bringing up their account on the computer in front of her.

Autumn stood abruptly. "We should probably come back some other time. You're so busy with everything else right now that we don't wanna interfere. We're just getting ideas right now, anyway." Simone stood along with Autumn as Sarah's mouth hung open in confusion.

"Yeah, we'll just circle back another time when things calm down here at the bank. We don't wanna add to your plate right now." Simone threw her hand out in front of her and offered it to Sarah.

Shaking Simone's hand as she shuffled away from her desk with them, Sarah abruptly answered, "All right, well, just let me know if you want to go over your numbers and some options. I'll be here." She hugged Autumn and waved as they walked toward the door.

The girls exchanged glances and headed out the door. Once they got into the fresh air, Simone started first.

"Well, well, well . . . It pays to have friends around town." Simone smirked at her cousin and noticed Autumn rubbing her forehead like the last time they were this close to city hall. "Whoa, don't start this again. Let's get you into the car and back to the Pine."

Autumn nodded and took her cousin's arm to make her way into the SUV. "Thanks. I don't know what happened, but as soon as we walked outside, I got dizzy."

Simone slammed the passenger door and jogged around the other side to start the car. "It's okay. We're getting out of here." She drove the long way around several blocks to avoid driving past city hall on the way back to Parchment and Pine. Parking at the rear of the building, Simone turned to her cousin again. "You okay?"

With a long sigh, Autumn stared at the back of the shop and replied, "Yeah, I am now. Thanks for that." She thought for a moment and turned toward her cousin. "It was worth it to find out about the land acquisitions and the resource management company."

"At least now we know deals are being done for all that property, and it's a safe bet it isn't to put in more fairgrounds." Simone brushed her hand through her hair. "They're gonna drill on the land, aren't they?"

Autumn wrapped her scarf closer around her neck and breathed into it. "I think so, and even if it's against current regulations, something tells me the county commissioner will push it through one way or another." She grabbed her backpack on the floor beside her and saw her phone buzzing inside of it. Bending over to pull it out, she squinted at the caller. "Chief Walsh," she said as she clicked the button to accept the call. "Hello, Chief?"

Simone watched her cousin nod along as the chief spoke on the other end. As she tried to turn the engine off, Autumn put a hand on her arm and shook her head as a signal to keep it running.

"What's going on?" Simone asked as Autumn hung up the phone.

"The chief called from the local law office. Apparently Ayla filed her divorce papers only a couple weeks ago, but they got lost in the recent break-in. They weren't sure if they should continue processing them if she was still a missing person. The chief wanted us to come down there and talk with the lawyers." Autumn pulled her seatbelt back across her lap and readjusted herself for the ride.

"He wants us to talk to them? What for? She's here, isn't she? Let Ayla deal with the final paperwork and her returning ex." Simone backed up the car and headed for the law office. "Unless . . . you and the chief both think something's wrong with Ayla?"

Autumn peered out the window as they drove further away from Main Street. "Wrong with Ayla? Definitely. With these divorce papers going missing just after her ex resurfaces? I think we better go find out."

CHAPTER 21

Simone walked through the law office entrance with Autumn close behind her. Immediately, she saw Ben standing at the end of a hallway with his father and talking to several employees behind him.

Ben sighed and walked over to the girls, putting his hand on Simone's shoulder. "Thanks for coming. Dad wanted your take on Ayla." Ben turned to Autumn and tilted his head toward the hallway. "You better go back."

With a nod, Autumn headed for Chief Walsh. Simone followed as Ben grabbed her arm to pull her back for a moment.

"Hey, whatever's going on, I smell trouble," he whispered. "So please, don't go jumping into it with both feet, okay?

I'd like to have you around for more motorcycle rides and late-night coffee runs."

Simone smirked at him. "Oh, is that all I'm good for? Being a backseat rider and fetching coffee?"

Ben nodded at her and smiled. "I do like all those things . . . and more." He brought his mouth up to Simone's ear and whispered again. "Just keep your eyes and ears open on this one. I don't like where it's headed."

She met eyes with him and saw the seriousness in them now. Nodding, she turned to walk toward Autumn at the back of the hallway.

The chief nodded as Simone and Ben approached. "Simone, I told Autumn that Ayla made her wishes clear just recently by filing divorce papers. In the mountain region, you only need one party to start the process, so that was enough for the law firm to process the paperwork. But, with the break-in, a handful of files got taken, including that one."

"I don't understand, Chief." Simone looked at him in confusion. "Why can't they just continue processing the paperwork? What do you need us for?"

Chief Walsh sighed and glanced at Autumn. "Well, for one thing, the lawyers wondered if Ayla's still missing. And even though she came 'round the other day, I think we're all wondering if she was in her right mind."

Ben interjected, "Yeah, we were hoping you'd both shed some light on that for us. She gave some really strange answers to us when we talked, and the chief wanted to hear your take.

Plus . . ." Ben looked over at his father, wondering if he should continue.

The chief nodded in approval. "Go ahead. Let's see what they think."

A couple employees nudged past the chief in the hallway, and they all scooted out of the way while keeping quiet for a moment. Ben took the moment to squeeze past his father and head for the back wall of the office. He raised his finger toward a wall of employee photos and pointed to one familiar face that stood out.

"Just made partner." Ben looked up at the photo and then back at the girls. "Recognize the face?"

Autumn gasped and squinted at the chief. "Philip Gibson."

Simone inched closer to the photo to get a better look. "Ayla's dead neighbor?"

Chief Walsh moved in closer and confirmed. "That's right. I didn't know the man, but apparently he worked at a firm up in Blake County for many years, so it's no wonder."

"And now Ayla's dead neighbor worked here as a partner?" Autumn took a few steps to stand directly in front of the photo while she thought out loud. "Where her divorce papers were being processed . . . But they conveniently got stolen when she went missing and her ex showed up again."

"And Gibson was the one processing the divorce paper-work, but he put it on hold for quite some time until the firm just pushed it through." Ben crossed his arms over his chest as he spoke.

"Yet, when it got pushed through," Simone continued, "that's when the break-in happened? What else got stolen besides Ayla's divorce papers?"

"Yep, with all the files in the same file cabinet." The chief moved further into the back-office space and pointed at a tall filing cabinet standing on a back wall. "Mostly all family law stuff, but the largest file was Ayla's. And I'm inclined to believe there's a reason for that."

Autumn took a few steps around the office, trying to piece things together. "Why would Mr. Gibson put a hold on the divorce papers? Sorcha said Ayla was finally ready to let Brodie go."

Simone shrugged, following her cousin's train of thought. "It's easy to have second thoughts, especially after being married to someone for years, I'd imagine." She looked over at Ben. "I'm just guessing."

The chief glanced down at the floor as Autumn moved around the office. "Autumn, you're trekking a bunch of rocks around."

Lifting the heel of one boot, Autumn looked down to check. "Oh shoot, I'm sorry. I didn't mean to make a mess of their office."

Chief Walsh shook his head at her and lifted a hand in the air for her to stop. "No, that's not what I mean." He bent down and grabbed a few of the rocky pebbles from the floor before glancing up at Ben. "Shale stone. It's the same."

Simone moved her eyes between both men. "Same as what?"

Standing and brushing his palms together to dust them off, the chief sighed. "Let's go outside and talk, shall we?" He raised his hand and motioned for them all to leave the office.

One by one, they each walked through the small hallway toward the front lobby again. The chief tipped his hat at the desk clerk. "I'll be back in a minute."

Ben held the door open for them and a few other employees who headed out. They made their way toward the police car parked in the side lot and then circled up.

"Now, Autumn," the chief started, "why don't you tell me where you've been to get all those rocks in your boots?"

Autumn cinched her coat up tighter and looked down at her boots again. "It's from Ayla's, Chief. I've gone over there a couple times now and . . ." She paused, realizing he probably wouldn't like that the girls had been back to the property since the day she found the body.

Chief Walsh rubbed his face with his hand and then nodded. "Go on. Don't stop now."

"Well, it's so rocky over there, and the day that James and I found Mr. Gibson, we walked down by the water where it was sandy. I haven't been able to get all of that out of my boots yet." Autumn shrugged. "I've been trying to, but it just comes out all over the place." As soon as she said the words, a thought sparked in her mind. "It's related to the break-in, isn't it?"

Crouching down, the chief motioned for Autumn to do the same. "Sit down for me, will you?" As Autumn sat, he grabbed a small knife from his pants pocket and began scraping at the bottom of her boot. He held up a few pieces of rock in his hand again. "I'm willing to bet that these pieces match what we pulled from the floor in the law office the day after the break-in. There was rocky mud everywhere."

"Yeah, and half of a very large boot print along with them." Ben squinted at his father. "Want me to get a warrant?"

The girls both looked at Chief Walsh, wondering what his next step would be.

"Yep." The chief nodded. "And put a rush on it. I'm betting if we head over there this afternoon, we may just catch him unsuspecting."

Autumn wrapped her arms around her bent knees and met eyes with the chief as she received another insight. "And maybe in the middle of something even bigger."

CHAPTER 22

Simone creeped along the side of her SUV with Autumn as they scoped out Ayla's property from down the road. Autumn waved her hand for Simone to keep coming.

"Someone else is here with Brodie. I see two trucks parked toward the back of the driveway." Autumn quickened her pace as she walked through the rocky woods next door to the home.

The girls eased their way around the side of the house, being careful not to attract attention. A couple men stood on the far side of the lot near the driveway. Autumn peeked her head around the corner of the house and listened as the men began shouting at one another.

"I've had it, Brodie! This is our chance now that you're back in with Ayla. Craig's already got the county financing tied down, so we just have to deliver on the land. Now that Phil's gone, they want all of mama's property . . . and this one." The man paced back and forth and chewed on a long blade of grass between his teeth. "That'll set us up rather nicely for the long haul."

Autumn leaned down to whisper to Simone, who peered her head around the corner beneath Autumn's. "That must be Brodie's brother. Mrs. Leslie mentioned they'd been bickering about the land."

Simone nodded and focused on the two men. "They both have the aura of greed around them. And who knows what somebody would do if they're greedy enough." The girls listened intently again as the men went on.

"Are you saying you had something to do with Phil dying? Because if you did, so help me, Dunn Aitken . . ." Brodie raised his fist in the air at his brother and moved closer to him.

"Relax, Brodie! I didn't have nothin' to do with that, swear it. I know he helped get Ayla on our good side. Besides, he was part of the deal, too. If it weren't for him, we wouldn't have enough land to sweeten the deal and get all of this lawyer nonsense done." Dunn kicked a pile of rocks with his boot. "Shesh, next thing you know, you'll be thinking I'm turning on you . . . my own brother."

Brodie gave him the eye just as a buzz came from the side of the house where the girls stood watching. Autumn quickly grabbed at her coat pocket and pulled out her phone to find a message from the chief reading, *Got the warrant. Don't go over there on your own.*

Autumn huffed under her breath. "A little late for that."

"Who's there?" Brodie yelled as he turned and started approaching the house. "I said, who's there?" he yelled even louder.

Dunn walked briskly to the back of his truck, pulled down the tailgate, and grabbed a rifle. He immediately cocked it and met his brother, aiming the gun toward the house. "Y'all better come out now before I start shootin'."

Autumn eyed Simone and nodded. "We need more information." Autumn moved away from the side wall and outstretched her hands at her sides.

Simone stayed behind the wall and whispered, "I like our odds." She smirked and glanced around the property as Autumn inched out in the clearing.

"You?" Brodie moved a step closer. "Didn't I see you with Ayla's sister at the coffee shop? What're you doing here?"

Giving them an innocent look, Autumn shrugged. "We're all so concerned about Ayla. I wanted to check and make sure she was okay after coming back so suddenly. I was hoping to stop by and give her some company."

"Well, she ain't here!" Dunn yelled as he lifted the barrel of the shotgun a little higher. "And this here is private property, so you best be on your way." He waved the gun toward the house to signal her to leave.

Autumn turned toward Brodie for a moment, trying to read his thoughts. "I just wanted to be sure she was okay and had company."

Brodie squinted at her and stepped closer. "Wait a minute. Aren't you the one I saw in the paper, the one who found Philip? You were on the property before."

As Brodie spoke, Dunn took aim at Autumn with the rifle. "Well, well, well . . ." Dunn smiled from behind the gun barrel. "Looks like we have ourselves a little snoop. And I don't like snoops."

With his words, a trembling sound came from the ground beneath them. Autumn felt a strange pressure rising below them before a geyser of water burst through the ground, sending broken pipe pieces through the air.

Autumn ducked and covered her head, and Simone walked out from behind the house with a focused expression on her face. The two men ducked and ran toward Dunn's truck.

"You're not going anywhere." Autumn lifted her hands high at her sides and spoke to the elements. "Winds of these lands, move swiftly. Form a funnel. Barricade them in." The winds howled around them and blew the spraying water across the back of the property. Rocks drew up from the ground into a funnel shape around Dunn's truck, encapsulating them in one place.

Both men strained to keep their eyes open while using their hands to block their faces. Dunn dropped the rifle as he cowered behind his forearms. "Make them stop, Brodie."

"Just tell us your plan and what happened to Ayla. Then we'll leave," Autumn yelled into the wind at them.

Dunn whimpered and crouched down on the ground beside the truck tire. "Make them stop."

Brodie closed his eyes and tightened his fists. Autumn watched curiously as he punched his hands down firmly with a loud groan. Suddenly, piece by piece, a section of rocks fell from the funnel surrounding them. A large thud rang through the property as they dropped, and Brodie inched his way through the broken funnel.

Simone's mouth dropped open as she stared at the man walking through wind, rock, and water. "Whoa, I wasn't expecting that."

Brodie brushed his hand over the top of his head to remove a bunch of rubble. "Ayla isn't the only one around here with abilities." He crouched down on the ground to lift a large boulder the size of a truck tire between his arms. Looking directly at the girls, he asked firmly, "Who wants to see how far mine can go?"

Jo's Full Moon Gratitude Bath

On the night of the full moon, or sometime during the three days before and after, take some time for a gratitude bath. Draw a moderate temperature bath and sprinkle the following ingredients into the water as it fills:

2 Tbsp rose petals or dried rose hips

2 Tbsp hibiscus flowers, dried or fresh

3-5 drops bergamot essential oil

Add several pink or green crystals around the outer edge of the tub. Step into the filled bath as you recite the words:

*Abundance surrounds me. I am filled with gratitude for all that
I have.*

Place both of your hands on your heart center and breathe
deeply for three full breaths. Soak for at least ten minutes
before draining the water.

CHAPTER 23

Autumn and Simone dove away from each other as Brodie hurled the boulder around his body and flung it through the air. Autumn panted as she recomposed herself and stood up to summon the winds again.

"Fly fast. Fly with force." With a thrashing of her arms to one side, a massive hurricane-strength wind forced its way through the property toward Brodie and knocked him to the ground. "Why did you break into the law office if Philip was helping you?"

Brodie shook off the force and picked himself up. He looked back at his brother huddled beside the truck in fear and then toward Autumn. "Those divorce papers were never supposed to go through. I needed this property, and when somebody killed Phil, well . . ."

"You had to make sure you still had rights to this place by destroying those papers." Simone glared at him as she positioned her feet firmly in place and lifted an arm to the side, ready to react.

The gushing water subsided behind Brodie as Simone calmed her energy and listened to his explanation. His chest heaved as he panted and looked around at the mess. Shaking his head, he appeared defeated. "This land may be my last chance to make something of myself."

Autumn and Simone exchanged looks and dropped their arms. With a sense of knowing that the man had little left in him, Autumn approached him. "You wanted to make money from the resources of the land."

He nodded in agreement. "My brother got the deal underway for my mother's property, and I went along with it. I knew Ayla never would go for it, though."

"Especially not once you divorced." Autumn eyed him sympathetically. She sensed a power in him overridden by sincerity. "You still love her."

"I do. Of course I do." Brodie threw his hands up in the air, and Autumn and Simone took a few steps back out of caution. "She's been my world for twenty years, but I know I'm no good for her."

A distinct gun-cocking noise came from nearby the house, and Autumn turned to see Chief Walsh and Ben with guns raised.

"Step away from the girls and put your hands up." The chief glared at Brodie while Ben kicked the rifle away from beside Dunn on the ground.

Chief Walsh waved one hand over his head as a flood of officers ran past him to grab Brodie and Dunn. He holstered his weapon and eyed the girls with frustration. "Had to go ahead of us, didn't you? You all right?"

Autumn nodded and walked over to him in relief. "Yeah, we're fine. They confessed to the break-in and to being part of the fracking ring."

The chief looked over at Brodie being handcuffed and pulled some papers from his cargo pants pocket. "A warrant to search the property. I'm sure if we check your boots, they'll be a match to the prints found at the law firm as well. And along with the fracking, you've got some hefty charges there." Turning to Autumn and Simone, the chief questioned, "Any reason we need to add murder or kidnapping to that list?"

Brodie lifted his head abruptly at Autumn and widened his eyes. "I didn't—"

"No, Chief. He's not the one we're looking for, and neither is his brother." Autumn moved around the property as she spoke, catching a potent scent of thyme wafting through the air just as it had the day she and James walked the property.

"Chief! Over here!" one of the county officers called out to Chief Walsh. He held up a gloved hand holding burnt remnants of paper. "Looks like we have some missing documents from the law firm."

Simone glanced over at Ben with a tight-lipped smile before walking over to Autumn. Simone put her hand on her cousin's shoulder. "What do you think?"

A strong breeze blew through Autumn's hair, lifting it in the direction of the woods that lined the property. "I think . . . we've been missing something that's been right in front of us all along."

Following Autumn's gaze out to the trees, Simone squinted. "There's that purple haze again."

"Mm-hmm. And where there's purple haze . . ." Autumn turned and jogged back to a squad car where an officer placed Brodie inside with his brother. She put her hand on the officer's arm and looked kindly into his eyes. "Give me a minute, would you?"

The officer paused for a moment and smiled. "All right, ma'am." He stepped aside to let Autumn talk with Brodie.

She bent down beside the police car door to meet Brodie where he sat inside the car. "If you still love her, then tell me what you see in her now." She waited patiently as Brodie sat staring at the floor of the police car.

He sighed and shook his head. "She's not the same. I honestly don't know where she was, but wherever it was, it changed her. Heck, she barely remembered me when she showed up the other night. And then to just take me back like I'd done nothin' wrong." Brodie sighed. "Even after putting up with me for twenty years, she always gave me what-for when I came crawling back." He raised his head to look straight into Autumn's eyes. "To heck with the land. I should have known that deal would never go through. But Ayla . . . You find out what's happened, and you bring her back to her old self, you hear?"

Autumn nodded as she stood up from the ground. "I will. I promise you I will." She turned to walk back toward Simone as several county police officers huddled up by the vehicle.

Simone locked arms with her cousin and leaned in close to whisper as they walked away, "Find out anything?"

"He sensed it, too. Ayla's not herself." Autumn stopped in front of Ayla's home and looked up at the front porch to gain some insight.

"Well, we figured that. Did he say what happened to her?" Simone looked over the front of the house just as Autumn did but saw nothing but battered shutters and chipped paint.

"No, but . . ." Autumn's eyes stopped as she saw something in the sky above the home. Her necklace warmed at her chest, and she placed a hand over it to receive greater awareness from its energy. With her other hand, she pointed up to a crescent moon hanging over the peak of the home. "If the pieces I'm putting together are correct, I know a way that we can find out for sure."

CHAPTER 24

Autumn peered out the front window of Parchment and Pine as she pulled on her wool coat. Simone peeked over her shoulder to look down Main Street.

"Did you call everyone?" Simone asked.

"Yeah, they're all onboard. Jo and Sorcha have Ayla at the shop now." Autumn scooped her long hair out of her coat collar and wrapped her knit scarf around her neck.

"Are you sure you wanna do this?" Simone gave her cousin the eye. "You can stay at the shop, and we can all do this without putting you at risk."

Shaking her head, Autumn walked to the front door as Tavish trotted up beside her feet. "No, I'm going. I need to be sure, and besides, we need to have some sort of comparison to work with." Autumn bent down and gave Tavish a head scratch. "Aw, cutie. You stay here, okay? Don't worry, I'll be fine."

Tavish rubbed his head on Autumn's leg and meowed loudly before standing in front of the door.

Simone smirked at the cat. "Looks like he agrees with me."

Autumn sighed and snatched him up in her arms. "Sorry, Tav. Not today. We'll be back before you know it."

Simone grabbed her coat off the wall hook and followed Autumn out the front door, shrugging at the cat as he jumped into the front window. "Better luck next time," she told him as she closed the door.

"There they are." Autumn pointed to Jo, Penny, Sorcha, and Ayla coming out of Jo's bath shop a block away on Main Street.

"Okay, so what do you wanna do? Follow close behind?" Simone zipped her quilted coat up all the way so the collar stood straight around her neck. She shoved her hands into her pockets and proceeded down the street with Autumn.

"Yeah, let's just keep our distance and watch. We know where they're headed, so I wanna see what happens as we get closer." Autumn waved to a few locals passing by on the sidewalk but kept her attention on the group of women.

The girls watched from afar as Jo pointed out the new year banners hanging from the light poles with illustrated images of majestic stags. They could see the others chatting away as Ayla appeared bored from the scene. As they continued walking, Penny led them down another block before reaching the corner to turn toward city hall.

The bell rang out loudly throughout town, and Autumn felt the energy draining from her chest. She breathed deeply to keep up her strength as she watched the others.

Simone put her arm around her cousin to help prop her up. "Just stay strong. You can do this."

Across the street, the girls watched as Ayla put her hands to her head and fell to the ground. Jo and Penny rushed to her side, but Sorcha stared at her sister with an expression of anger.

"I'm calling Ben." Simone pulled her phone out of her pocket and messaged him as she crossed the street with Autumn, holding her cousin up with her other arm. "They're on the way now."

As the girls met up with the group, Ayla began writhing furiously on the ground.

"What is that horrid sound?" she screeched, and covered her ears. "My head is pounding! And my energy . . ." Ayla balled herself up into the fetal position on the ground as Chief Ian Walsh, Ben, and a couple officers rushed across the street at them.

As soon as the officers came forward, Penny backed away in search of Autumn, who stood steadying herself against Simone while drained of all color. "Oh dear, you were right. The bell affected her, but I'm afraid of what it's doing to you as well."

"We've got her," the chief called as he grabbed Ayla from the sidewalk and hoisted her up into the other officers' arms. "Take her back to the station and put her in a holding cell until I get there."

"Yes, Chief." The officers nodded and dragged Ayla back to the station behind city hall.

He walked toward Autumn and offered his arm instead of Simone's. "Let's get you back to the station as well. No need to show us how strong you are."

Autumn folded in half as the chief caught her before she fell onto the sidewalk. "Chief, I can't make it."

"Nonsense. If I know you, you've got more fight in you than the entire mountain region put together . . . just like the rest of your family." The chief glanced over at Jo as he carried Autumn across the street under his arm.

They made their way to the police station, and Ian escorted them through a side door. "Now then, we'll head down to the holding cells to get some answers. But first, I'll have someone bring you some water." The chief raised Autumn's chin with his hand and assessed her condition. "To be on the safe side, we better get her some attention. My men are well-trained for emergencies. I'll call Ben down."

Jo put a hand on Ian's arm. "No need. My sister will do better for her than anyone else could."

Penny nodded and took her daughter's hand in hers as the chief positioned Autumn on a bench in the back of the station.

"Just keep watch while I work." Penny pulled the locket out from under her daughter's coat. She ran her hand over the tree root emblem fused to the locket, and it slowly shimmered with golden light.

Smiling, Penny rocked back and forth and channeled her gifts. "Powers of the earth, overcome this blight. Heal, restore, and leave no effects in sight." She pressed the locket against Autumn's skin. "Let the one who wields the four elements reclaim her energy and take up her mantle once again."

Autumn sucked in a deep breath at Penny's last words. She sat up abruptly and looked directly into her mother's eyes. "It's okay. I feel the energy running through me again."

Her mother sighed in relief and gently tucked the locket back into Autumn's coat. "My ladybug, you are so strong."

The chief widened his eyes and exchanged a glance with Ben beside him. "Well, that was something."

Shaking his head, Ben rubbed the back of his neck with his hand. "I'm glad you're all on our side."

Jo waved her hand through the air. "Of course we are. Now, let's get down to business, shall we?" She moved down the hallway and headed for the stairs to the holding area. "Chief, we have some questioning to do."

Ian nodded and followed Jo, with Ben and Simone close behind them. "Yes, ma'am. Let's get to it. I'd like to figure out what exactly is going on here before I'm much older."

"I'll stay here with Autumn. Simone, go with them and use your intuition to help your mother." Penny grabbed Simone's hand and gave her an anxious smile.

Jo led the way down the stairs toward the cell where a very upset Ayla sat flailing around on a cold concrete floor. As soon as she saw them come in, she wrapped her arms around her knees and turned her back.

"Now, Ayla, we're going to ask you some questions, and you need to give us some straight answers." The chief had a layered aura around him of bright red and yellow hues that Simone distinctly felt as serious determination. He aimed to get answers out of this woman one way or another.

Stepping forward and placing her hands on the bars, Jo sent golden shimmers across the bars of the cell. "Shall we call you Ayla? Or is there a different name you prefer?"

Simone watched as her mother took a small vile from her patch pocket and held it up in her fingers. "Moon water," Simone whispered to Ben beside her.

Ayla peeked her eyes slightly over her arms to see Jo's actions. "Ciarra," she said curtly.

Jo opened the vile and splashed a few drops into her palm before circling a finger through the drops. "Ciarra . . . the name of dusk. Mmmm, the rise of the moon and the fading of the sun."

"What is this horrid feeling?" Shaking in pain, the one preferring to be named Ciarra lifted her head, looking directly at Jo now. "Why do I feel my energy fading?"

"Well, Ciarra, I can help you if you help me." Jo raised an eyebrow at her as she glanced into the water droplets within her palm. "You are not from this land, are you?"

Ciarra laughed at the question. "This is only temporary, but I was promised a safe haven. A land away from the dark. But you people lack energy. You're constrained by time and space, and this place became exhausting some time ago." She moaned through the pain and grabbed at her head. "What's happening to me?"

"Ah, yes. That would be the iron bell in our town square. You see, we chose long ago to protect our town from outside harm. And for us, at the time, that meant the fae." Jo dipped one fingertip into the water droplets and held it up between the cell bars between her and Ayla.

Ben leaned over to Simone's ear. "The fae? Does she mean, like, fairies?"

Simone tilted her head at Ben and gave him a smirk to signify how adorably naive he sounded. "Just listen."

"Those who feel the effects of the iron show themselves to be of a different realm. And you, Ciarra, have proven yourself to be just that." Jo poured several more drops of water from the vile into her palm and lifted it toward her face. She began walking along the cell bars and eyeing Ciarra in between glances at her palm. "Waters of these lands reveal what lies beneath the surface. Show us the true nature of those in the shadows. Break the spell of concealment and bring all to light."

Jo turned abruptly at footsteps coming down the stairs and found Autumn and Penny walking into the room. The locket around Autumn's neck glowed brightly with emerald-green light, and she practically hovered over to Jo's position in front of the cell.

"She felt your spell from upstairs," Penny explained. "The energy began coursing through her again, and I couldn't stop her from coming down to help."

Autumn took hold of Jo's free hand and nodded to Simone to join them as well. "By the power of three, so shall it be."

The golden shimmers surrounding the cell bars shined even brighter now as the three women locked hands and channeled their gifts. The small puddle of water within Jo's hand swirled as if a whirlpool had activated. They stared at Ciarra on the floor of the cell as her appearance slowly faded from that of Ayla to one of a haggard older woman with gray hair and sagging skin.

"I'm barely the fae I once was." The one they once looked at as Ayla now stumbled to her feet, holding herself up by the side wall. "Thousands of years of darkness, even with powerful magic, can make one long for brighter days. So, I accepted the offer to exchange a life in the dark for a shorter one in the light."

"Who offered this to you? How was this exchange done?" Jo circled her palm in the air to continue the whirlpool within it.

Ciarra laughed as she thought but buckled over at the waist in pain. "Ayla was only the pawn in our game. Her energy connected to mine through light and dark within our multidimensional lives. She is me, and I am her, on different wavelengths and in different worlds. But the one who made the connection . . . goes by the name of Delia. The one of the moon and the hunt. She crossed dreamworlds with her potions and offered me a chance at a new life."

"Delia." Autumn spoke her name aloud again to confirm it. "So she got you here through the portal in the woods on Ayla's property. And you assumed Ayla's identity."

"Funny what you can do when the moon activates a portal between worlds. You can turn dreamwork into reality. Thoughts into channeled communication. And intention into shapeshifting." Ciarra stumbled over to the cell bars directly in front of them and locked eyes with Penny. "You know of what I speak."

Penny swallowed hard and met Ciarra's gaze. "The potion Delia used worked through dreamwork and channeled letters. The ones with the lunar symbol on them."

The edge of Ciarra's mouth lifted in a slight smile. She liked the idea of someone finally appreciating her magic. "We exchanged letters since she preferred to work in shadow. So, once I got to these lands on the night of the eclipse, we used the letters for communication. Of course, the shapeshifting came easy for a dark fae such as myself, and I finally felt free to roam untethered. I just didn't expect to be summoned back to actually become Ayla for a while, but I suppose it was necessary to complete the ruse."

"So you agreed to become Ayla in the hope of taking over her body and living freely around our lands." Penny glared at Ciarra as if she embodied everything Penny had fought against for so long. "Just as any dark fae does to dominate other lands and beings. You're disgusting."

Autumn stepped forward and distracted Ciarra from Penny's gaze. "All right, if you are here, then where is Ayla?"

Ciarra shrugged and then winced in pain. "Make the pain stop and I will tell you."

"There's no need," Jo replied. "I know where she is."

Autumn turned to her aunt and searched her eyes for the answer. "The portal."

"It was an even trade," Ciarra noted. "A being in one land for a being in another. The way I see it, she gets a much longer life in my lands, albeit dark."

"That tells us where Ayla is, but what about Philip Gibson?" Simone stared at Ciarra, trying to figure out how he fit in.

"Gibson?" Ciarra tilted her head in thought. "You mean that useless man trying to interfere with the exchange? Yes . . . He needed to be dealt with. I had a small window for the portal during the eclipse, and he got in the way. It was his fault, really, in not knowing what he was dealing with, so I disposed of him."

The chief turned to Ben beside him. "We've heard enough. Ben, send some officers out to apprehend Delia and charge her with kidnapping. We'll hold this one here until we figure out how to send her back to where she came from."

"Got it, Chief." Ben headed up the stairs as the others re-grouped.

Simone lifted her hands at her sides. "How do we get Ayla back from the portal?"

Jo walked over beside Penny and opened her palm wider for her sister to see. She scooped the remaining water from her palm with the other hand, and it rose into a swirling donut shape into the air above her hand. Jo watched for Penny to make a realization.

Penny gasped and met eyes with Jo. "You're a genius, Josephine MacKinnon. The mountain hag stone."

CHAPTER 25

Eve knocked on the door to the girls' cottage and bounced on her tiptoes as she waited.

Lainy sighed and rolled her eyes beside Eve. "Would you stop fidgeting? Use some of that earth energy to calm down."

Simone opened the door and let Eve and Lainy inside. "Come on in. We're just getting started."

Eve turned her head toward Lainy as she walked in. "I'm just excited, and fidgeting helps." She shrugged as Lainy let a tiny smile creep over her lips.

The two of them threw their coats over a hook at the entry and walked into the living room where Autumn, Simone, Jo, and Penny gathered.

"Oh, girls!" Jo lifted a hand to wave them over. "You're just in time. Now, our ancestors have passed down many magical tools through the MacKinnon line, and tonight we're going to retrieve one of those tools."

"We believe it'll help us open the portal to the fae world and find Ayla," Autumn explained.

"That's right," Penny continued. "The tool we seek is the one water forged from the earth. It is the mountain hag stone that our ancestors retrieved near a portal in the region. It's said to be from the time of the great floods, fires, and earthquakes that plagued the region."

Jo lit a tall blue taper candle in the center of the coffee table and placed two large blue azurite crystals on either side of it. "Hag stones serve as elemental portals to other worlds. Even if there is no lunar eclipse to activate the opening, we can use a hag stone to create the same doorway. The water that forged the hole serves as the energetic connection. The earth holds the realities in place on either side."

"So, Eve and Simone, you're both center stage on this one." Autumn pulled Eve's sleeve to get her to stand near the center of the coffee table.

"Oh, okay. I guess I can do that." Eve shrugged. "This is so weird because I've had the strangest pull toward making all kinds of donuts lately. It's like every time I head into the kitchen, donut recipes seem to fall open from my recipe books, and I've had such a hankering for donuts! And now, we're trying to retrieve a donut-shaped stone portal. How crazy is that?"

Simone laughed as she moved closer beside Eve alongside the coffee table. "So your insight works through your belly, huh? That's one way to do it."

Eve gave them all a bashful grin. "It's just the way I'm programmed, I guess."

Penny nodded from across the table. "That's a perfectly good way to use sensations for intuitive understanding, Eve. And now that you know those hunger pangs hold a connection, you can watch for them in the future as well." She smiled at Eve reassuringly.

"Thanks, Penny." Eve perked up at the idea.

"All right, then. We don't have all night. Everyone, lock hands." Jo grabbed hands with Penny and Lainy beside her, and the others did the same. "Set your intention for the wardrobe key to reveal itself in Autumn's locket. From there, we can retrieve the hag stone to open the portal. Our goal is to get the stone and get Ayla back." They all nodded, and Jo continued. "Autumn, please lead the spell."

Taking a deep breath and closing her eyes, Autumn focused on their intention just as Tavish popped up beside her in the circle. "Ancestors and elements of earth, air, fire, and water, we call upon you now for support. Allow us to use your strength and resources to restore balance to this land and that of the portal. Bring the mountain hag stone to light so that we may find Ayla within our sight. Earth and water as one, reveal the key. As I say it, so shall it be."

A soft whispering grew around them in the room, and Autumn's necklace shone with brilliant green light at her chest. She placed a hand on the locket to sense if something was lying within it. Tavish brushed against her leg and purred as she checked.

Smiling at her successful spell, Autumn opened the locket to reveal the tiny antique key that had opened Gran's heirloom wardrobe several times before. "Got it."

Autumn went to the tall wooden wardrobe standing on the living room wall behind the entry door. She placed the key inside the lock and opened the double doors to find the antique chest glowing with emerald light at the bottom of the wardrobe. Carefully, she opened the chest and peered inside.

"Sim," she called as she pulled out an odd-shaped but flattened gray rock with a hole through the center. "Take this." Handing the stone to Simone, Autumn returned the chest and the wardrobe to its normal state.

Simone held the stone up, flipped it around in her fingers, and looked through the center hole. "It's just a stone, but . . . I see glints of something within the hole. Purple flashes."

"Don't look too closely until we've arrived at the portal," Jo suggested. "A witch would be wise to always anchor her energy before connecting with what lies within the hag stone. You don't want to lose yourself to another world."

Looking seriously at her mother, Simone nodded and placed the stone down on the coffee table. "Let's just finish this up and get going."

"Right." Autumn grabbed hands with Simone and Eve. The others followed to make a circle once again. "Ancestors and elements, we thank you for allowing us to retrieve this stone. Support us in our endeavors as we bring back our friend from the world unknown. As I say it, so shall it be."

They dropped hands and looked around the circle as Jo blew out the candle. Tavish jumped up on the coffee table and nudged the stone across the surface with his nose.

Eyeing it on the table, Simone sighed. "Are we ready for this?"

Autumn snatched up the hag stone, headed to the door, and shrugged. "Only one way to find out."

CHAPTER 26

Autumn looked around Ayla's dark property before rubbing her palms together and bringing them to her mouth. She exhaled into them as she thought of Ciarra taking Ayla. As the anger bubbled up inside her, a flame sparked within her palms. She opened her hands as the other coven members and the girls' mothers looked on at the light appearing before them.

"We're going to get her back," Autumn said as she lifted the flame in front of her.

"Yes, we are. I have every confidence." Jo smiled before a few footsteps cracked over the rocks behind her. "Oh, James! There you are! And Ben, we didn't expect you this evening. Oh dear, and I see you've brought Ciarra with you." Jo stared at Ben in surprise as he held a handcuffed Ciarra firmly with one arm.

"He wouldn't take no for an answer." James hugged Autumn as he carefully steered clear of her flaming palms. "Looks like you've started without us."

Simone's mouth dropped open as she looked at Ben. "What're you doing here?"

Ben threw his hands up in front of him in neutrality. "Dad and I agreed that if anyone spotted you on the property of a recent murder investigation, you'd need a police officer with you to ease the tension. Anyway, Ciarra needed to be returned to where she belongs and . . . To be honest, I didn't want you out here without James and me both."

Crossing her arms at her chest, Simone stood staring at him in silence for a moment. "Fine. You can stay, but don't even think about getting in the way."

He dipped his head to the side and raised his eyebrows at her. "I don't think I could even if I tried."

"All right, everyone." Jo motioned for them all to come in close. "We need to walk out to the tree line. Autumn, you saw the hawthorn tree out near the water, correct?"

Autumn nodded at her aunt. "That's right. It's a ways out near the water's edge. We should keep an eye out for anything strange as we head out there."

Ciarra sighed. "This entire land seems strange, if you ask me." She stumbled as Ben continued pulling her further along.

"We didn't," Lainy replied as she moved beside Autumn and used the flame in Autumn's hand to ignite her own. "I'll light the rear of the group if you go in front," she suggested.

Following Autumn, they all walked quietly into the night through the rocky land. Eve and Penny scanned the landscape while Jo and Simone kept their focus on the water that lay ahead. Simone sensed the rapids pulling at the shore in the distance, and the hag stone in her pocket felt like a magnet drawing her toward them.

James walked beside Autumn as they continued. Halfway to the water, James took a step and heard a loud pop beneath his boot. He stopped to lift his foot as Autumn brought the flame closer.

Ben quickened his pace to catch up. "What is it?" He leaned over James's boot as they both pulled a shiny silver object from the treads.

"Looks like . . . a cufflink?" James scratched his head as he held the object between his fingers for Ben to see. "Who would wear cufflinks out here?"

Autumn moved the flame closer and eyed the four-leaf clover design as she recalled where she had seen it before. "A very greedy commissioner, that's who."

Exchanging glances with Simone, Autumn thought of Commissioner Craig leaving the fairgrounds office in anger. She had glimpsed the commissioner's very distinctive cufflinks peeking out of his jacket when he'd stormed past the girls.

"The guy who's been going around town trying to get money for fracking?" Simone questioned, leading Ben to turn his gaze at her.

"Yep, that's the one." Autumn nodded. "And the same one I saw suspiciously running into Delia Hall and Ciarra on Main Street the day Ayla seemed to reappear." Autumn turned toward Ciarra, who immediately looked the other way to avoid interrogation. "He acted taken aback to see them and then immediately turned to head the other way."

"I'm sending this to my dad. He'll wanna know about this." Ben took out his phone, snapped a picture of the cufflink, and started messaging Chief Walsh. A text immediately pinged in reply. "Oh, this thing goes deeper than we thought."

Autumn squinted at him curiously. "He already knew."

Ben nodded. "Yeah, apparently Commissioner Craig planned this whole thing. In fact, as soon as they arrested Delia Hall, she threw him under the bus for the entire kidnapping. Chief says the commissioner paid her to get it done."

"Craig paid Delia to get Ayla out of the picture?" Simone said with surprise. "What was the purpose of that?"

Autumn started walking again as the others followed her. "This land is valuable to him just like it is to Brodie and his brother. They all wanted to get the fracking underway and get paid."

"And Delia wanted Ayla's spot at the festival and her book deal," Eve chimed in from the back of the group.

"That's right," Autumn agreed. "The commissioner would have known that since he oversaw the festival. When Simone and I were at the fairgrounds office, he was upset with Mr. Doyle for leaving Ayla's booth spot open for so long. Craig tried to force him to fill the spot, and he knew it would go to Delia next."

"So Craig used Delia since he knew she wanted Ayla out of the way, too. He was behind the whole thing just to get the land for fracking." Simone put the pieces together just as they approached the river's edge a few feet ahead of them.

"I think you've all nailed it from what my dad just relayed." Ben walked a few more steps and eyed the dark river water. "You never know what's under the surface."

Simone stepped up beside him. "That's why it pays to have a water witch by your side." She smirked at him and took the hag stone out of her pocket. "Now, let's get Ayla back."

"Right, then." Penny nodded and stood in front of the group. "I see the hawthorn tree beyond the tree line over there on the ridge. Autumn, James, you both go into the portal to get Ayla. Simone will open the bridge while Eve keeps it anchored on this side. The rest of us can lend extra energy to them and you."

"Got it, but I just have one question," James said, staring out into the distance at the hawthorn tree.

Autumn knew instantly what James's fear was. "What if we can't find her over there?"

Jo sighed and walked up to James to envelop him in a hug. "Oh, dear, I know you're worried for your aunt, but keep your focus. She sits on the other side. Of that, I'm confident. There's no way Ciarra would allow her to roam free. It would be too risky. Plus, if I know Ayla, she'd want to stay close to the portal and use every ounce of her magic to reopen it." Jo rubbed James's arms and gave him a sympathetic look. "Do what you must to find her."

"You'll both feel the pull of the portal if you're running out of time," Penny continued. "It gives a warning to those who have passed through."

Shaking her head, Autumn moved to the front of the group alongside James. "Okay, I'm ready. Let's start the spell."

Jo moved toward the edge of the river and waved Simone over. "We'll do it together, dear." She lifted her skirt so as not to get it wet as she crouched down. Washing both of her hands in the chilly river, Jo connected with the water's energy first, and then Simone mirrored her.

"Water within us, show us the unseen. Connect us with other worlds beyond our own. Open the portal and bridge between us and the one taken against her will." Jo swirled her hands in the water, and golden shimmers of magical light appeared below them.

Simone smiled as she mimicked her mother once again and then took the mountain hag stone out of her coat pocket. The hole in the stone shimmered with deep-purple flickers. "I can sense the opening." She looked over her shoulder into the woods. "The purple haze is overtaking the trees."

Penny tapped Jo on the shoulder. "That's our cue."

Jo and Simone got up from the water's edge and rounded up the rest of the group into a circle. "Hold tightly together. Eve, stay grounded to the land while Simone holds the portal open. Autumn, James, you must take Ciarra with you." Jo gave her niece a grave expression. She pulled her close into an embrace and whispered in Autumn's ear, "She is cunning, but you are wise. Remember your strengths."

Autumn stepped back and nodded to her aunt. "I will." She stepped forward as James took hold of Ciarra's arm from Ben.

"Here we go." James peered up the ridge where just a week ago he'd found Mr. Gibson's body. Swallowing hard, he glanced at the water as they walked toward the trees. "The water lives within you, Aunt Ayla. Be strong."

Ciarra laughed under her breath. "Your aunt Ayla and I have the same energy, you know. Are you sure you don't want to just keep me here in her place?"

James tightened his grip on Ciarra's arm. "You're nothing like my aunt Ayla. She has a kind heart that isn't tainted by shadow and greed." He dragged her up the rocky ridge onto the outcropping over the water. "You're almost back where you belong."

Moving up the ridge with ease for someone as old as Ciarra, she smirked at James. "Everyone has shadows. And as for where I belong, my energy spans multiple dimensions. This won't be the last you'll see of me."

"All right, I'm going first. James, follow Ciarra through." Autumn's eyes wandered to the bottom of the hawthorn tree where a patch of mushrooms lay. She brushed her boot across the tops of them and then refocused on the portal in front of her. A purple haze of light danced below the branches of the hawthorn tree, and she pressed her hand onto it. Ripples dispersed in concentric circles across the surface like water. Autumn gulped and stepped through the haze.

James shoved Ciarra forward. "You're next." He pushed at Ciarra's back as she walked through the light.

Glancing over her shoulder at him, she smirked and lifted her handcuffed hands behind her to run her fingernails across the hazy portal door. A tear formed in the light opening and allowed darkness to seep through it. James tried to crouch down and move through the bottom portion of the portal opening, but it was too small.

"What are you doing?" he yelled as Ciarra moved beyond the purple light.

"Creating an advantage," she called back to him through the torn opening.

James's shoulders fell as he tried to push through the torn portal once more but couldn't. Ciarra had already disappeared into the other side with Autumn, leaving him standing alone beside the hawthorn tree. He immediately raced out to the ridge and called the others. "Ciarra's gone in behind Autumn and torn the opening. What can I do?"

Jo opened her eyes and stepped back from the circle. She replaced her joined hands by moving Penny's and Lainy's together in front of her. "Simone, maintain the bridge. I will check with the water."

Hastily moving to the water's edge, Jo knelt and touched a finger to the surface. She scanned the waves, looking into them for a vision. "She's torn the opening from the other side, but ours remains. It's up to Autumn and Ayla now to find the water energy within themselves and repair their side of the bridge."

"But if our side is all right, then can't we still get through?" James panted as he questioned Jo. "I'm too big, but one of the girls would probably fit."

Penny shook her head and placed her hand on his arm. "No, James. Each side is like a gate. When Ciarra sliced that side of the portal, she essentially locked the gate from the other side. Autumn and Ayla must return on their own now."

James shook his head and ran his hands over his face. "No, there's gotta be a way to get through and help Autumn. Who knows what Ciarra is capable of over there." James took a few steps, pacing back and forth, before footsteps crunched through the rocky land in the distant darkness.

The entire group turned to look toward the noise. Ben grabbed for his holster at his waist as they waited, holding their breath. Lainy summoned the fire energy within her and focused on a few logs scattered across the sandy river's edge. Immediately, several logs sparked with flames and created a large enough light to scan the surrounding landscape.

Through the darkness, a familiar little cat hurdled through the rocky land in front of a woman adorned in a long black cape. She pulled the hood from her head to reveal the frazzled curls and dark skin of a shadowy hedge witch.

Simone pulled back from the circle and allowed her mother to take her place. "Lajla? What are you doing here? And why is Tavish with you?" Simone approached the woman as Ben continued eyeing her.

"Simone, who is this?" Ben kept his hand on his holster as he waited.

"I am Lajla. Simone visited my apothecary shop with the fae witch recently." She lifted her hand in Tavish's direction on the ground. "When this little one showed up on my doorstep this evening, I knew he belonged to her, and it was time for us to reconnect." She looked up at the night sky above them. "It is the night of the new moon, after all."

"But why would Tavish lead you here?" Eve wondered out loud.

Simone eyed the hedge witch's aura and saw a deepening shade of green. "You're making amends, and Tavish knows you can help us."

Lajla smiled and moved under Eve's arm into the center of their circle. "I am here to close the circle on what I started and to ask for repayment of my favor." She pulled out a large tincture bottle with the symbol of the lunar eclipse on the front.

Simone moved into the center of the circle and took the bottle from her. "The portal tore on the other side, so how do we get them back?" She shook the bottle in her hand. "What can this do for us?"

Lajla untied the neck of her cape and let it fall to the ground, revealing a beautiful shimmering black jumpsuit underneath. "The serum serves as a channeling tool. A radio signal of sorts. If you have the portal open on this side now, then you can speak to those on the other side with this. Give them insight. Give them energy. Give them . . . a matching connection."

Tavish walked along the inside of the circle, rubbing his head on each person's legs as Lajla spoke. The cat purred loudly as he moved around the full circle and then back to Simone in the center.

"We are the matching connection," Simone said with realization as she snatched Tavish up from the ground and looked around at each of them.

"Mmmm, yes. A coven holds a great deal of power. It's seemingly separate yet whole within itself." Lajla took the tincture bottle back from Simone and poured some of the liquid onto the ground in the center of the circle. "When one piece gets removed, it eventually finds its way back to the whole, as its energy never separated to begin with."

"So Autumn can still sense the elements within us." Lainy lifted her hands, intertwined with those on either side of her. The flames burning the logs at the water's edge rose higher and shone more light onto the water than before. "And she can use them to enhance the elements within herself."

Simone dropped Tavish to the ground again and sat beside him at the pool of liquid from the tincture. "Right, and we can create an open channel for her thoughts to flow to us as well. We've done it before—actually, me and her. So let's just see what happens."

"Okay, so what's the plan?" Eve steadied herself in place, keeping her feet rooted to the ground.

Lajla smoothed the legs of her jumpsuit and sat down on the ground across from Simone. She blew a breath into the tincture pool between them. "Focus your energy on the fae witch. Autumn, correct?"

Simone nodded and concentrated on the pool, keeping a soft gaze on the surface.

"Send her the strength of your elements. Carry the vibration through time and space until you feel it reaching her." Lajla blew another breath over the liquid and hummed quietly for a moment. "Do not allow imbalances to disturb your energy. Just send the elements through your heart center until you are sure that they've reached her."

Lajla reached her hands across the pool toward Simone, and Tavish nudged Simone's arm up to get her to comply.

"Okay, geez. I got it, Tav." Simone grasped Lajla's hands and watched as she lifted her head to the sky and swayed from side to side. "I feel Autumn on the other side. She's searching in the darkness, trying not to be seen."

"Has she found Ayla?" James asked hurriedly.

"I feel both of their energies there." Simone struggled to make sense of what was coming through. "But I don't think Autumn has her yet."

James buried his head in his arms and crouched to the ground as he tried to be patient. "With calm tides, strength endures. Autumn, hear my words."

"She does," Simone confirmed. "And I can see our vibrations. They're carrying colors of light into the woods. James, your navy-blue vibration trailed over the water and into the purple haze." Tavish jumped into Simone's lap as she watched the light display in front of her. "Lainy, your bright-yellow vibration moved through the air like a fiery dragon aimed at the hawthorn tree. And Eve, there's a shimmering holiday red streaming from your heart and bouncing along the ground into the woods."

Jo gasped as her daughter described the colors of the coven. She exchanged glances with Penny beside her and squeezed her sister's hand. "The coven is becoming one. And I sense Ayla's energy now. She's closer than she's been in a long time."

"Good," Lajla interjected. "Let the new moon serve as a beacon, summoning her to you." She drew a circle in the rocky sand beside her and filled it in with her fingers until it was dark.

"From shadow to light, bring them within sight," she chanted, and raised her hands to signal all of them to continue chanting along with her.

"From shadow to light, bring them within sight." They all recited the chant twice more as the tides beside them grew larger and quicker.

Lajla looked directly into Simone's eyes. "Send her the water spirit. Let it flow from within you."

Simone stood up and let her arms swing freely in a rippling motion. As she moved, the river water rose several feet and pushed its tides toward the woods before crashing against the ridge.

"Holy cow," Ben exclaimed as he watched the water crash and then turned back to confirm that Simone had caused it. "That water just raged against the cliff."

Jo smiled to herself and released Penny's hand. "I feel them nearby."

"It is done." Lajla moved her legs beneath her in a kneeling position and placed her forehead to the ground. "The elements supported us in our endeavor."

Tavish walked toward the tree line, gradually working up to a gallop. Simone raced after him as the dark-purple haze from the woods lightened to a softer shade of lavender.

The rest of the group watched as two shadowy figures joined and walked out of the woods. Stumbling, they made it past the tree line as the fires from the water's edge shone on their faces.

"They made it!" Jo exclaimed as she ran up with the others. Fully embracing Ayla, Jo kissed her friend's forehead. "We've been waiting for your return, sweet friend."

James held Autumn tightly, never wanting to let her go again. "You had me worried there for a minute."

She smiled up at him. "You, worried? I don't believe it." Nuzzling back into his chest, she breathed in his scent of cherry cordial and chestnuts. "Thank you for the calm and the strength. I needed them both in the darkness."

He met eyes with her and squinted. "You heard what I said?"

Autumn nodded. "Heard them, felt them. All of it. From all of you." She stepped back and looked around the group and then down at Tavish now beside her feet. "I felt the full energy of our coven. Without it, I couldn't have channeled the power to restore the tear Ciarra made. Especially not without the water and earth energy that grew stronger within me." Autumn turned to Lajla for a moment. "And I'm guessing we have you to thank for successfully getting us all through this."

Lajla looked up at the dark sky above. "It was time that I rebalanced the energies I had misused."

"From serving Delia?" Autumn wrapped her arms around her chest and huddled her chin into her collar to keep warm.

Nodding, Lajla took a few steps toward the water. "My father bound me long ago to repay my family's debt to hers."

"Well, it's time we remove that binding for good." Autumn stood beside Lajla and took the hedge witch's hands within hers. She looked into Lajla's eyes and saw a compassion and longing for healing lying deep within them. "Ties that bind shall now unwind. Mark all debts paid and to the ground have them laid."

Strong winds picked up around them, and Autumn's hair swirled furiously as she kept her eyes on Lajla. The river beside them crashed onto the shore and snuffed out a bonfire, only for it to be rekindled once more as the wave subsided.

Autumn recited the chant again and kept her focus. "Ties that bind shall now unwind." Her feet lifted from the ground, and Lajla rose along with her. The two of them spun in a gentle circle a few feet in the air as sand kicked up underneath them. "Ties that bind shall now unwind. As the powers of the witches and the fae flow through me, I speak these words from acceptance and reclamation of this spirit. Let none limit one. As I say it, so shall it be."

They spun down to the ground once more, and Lajla sat for a moment to sense the new, unencumbered energy within her. Embracing Autumn, she whispered, "You are truly the four-points witch." Then, she stepped back to look her up and down. "And the rightful heir to the fae throne."

With a grateful smile, Autumn turned to face the group in the light of a couple remaining fires. She walked over and grabbed Simone's hand, raising it in the air. "Long live the Hollow's Glenn witches."

"The Hollow's Glenn witches!" they all cheered before gathering together in a group embrace.

Autumn snatched Tavish up from the ground below her feet, and he craned his neck over her shoulder. "What is it, boy?"

She glanced around before her eye caught a hint of a tiny sapphire flash in the tree line over the ridge. She and the cat looked at one another, and Tavish rubbed his nose along hers. He looked into her eyes and meowed.

"Do you see what I see?" They both stared off into the distance before she whispered into the cat's ear. "Wisps."

CHAPTER 27

E ve raced down the front steps of the girls' cottage with a bushel full of oranges in her arms. She stumbled along the path into the sanctuary woods as Tavish quickly overtook her.

Laughing, she yelled, "I can't keep up with you, cat!"

Simone peeked her head out of the trees ahead. "Are you coming, or what? We're about to start."

"Yeah, I'm coming," Eve panted, and picked up the pace. She met Simone and Tavish at the large clearing in the trees where the girls usually practiced their magic.

"Finally." Simone grabbed the bushel from Eve's arms. "Let's get these around the bonfire so we can light everything up!"

The two girls made their way to the center of the clearing where Autumn, Lainy, Jo, and Penny had piled firewood high in preparation for the celebration.

"Oh, good! You're here." Penny pulled a few oranges out of the bushel and arranged them in a circle around the firewood. "These should do nicely to activate our abundance for the new year."

"I brought as many as I could find." Eve helped Penny place the oranges an even distance apart. "They're few and far between around town now. Everyone's snatching up oranges for their new year's events."

"Well, we appreciate your efforts to find them, Eve." Jo patted her on the back. "Thank you."

A voice chimed in from the pathway heading back to the house. "Did we miss anything?"

Autumn turned from rearranging the firewood to see James standing at the tree opening with his mother; his uncle, Dillon; and Ayla. She hurried to him and wrapped him in a hug. "Not yet, but you were cutting it close. We're about to start." She kissed his cheek and smiled before turning to his relatives. "It's so good to see you all here. Thank you for coming to celebrate with us!"

Ayla chuckled. "Oh, my dear, I'm the one who should thank you! If it weren't for you and your coven, I wouldn't be here to celebrate. And my brother, Dillon, either, from what I've heard about the past several months."

Autumn took Ayla's hands in her own and nodded. "We're just glad you're safe now and among family." She turned and lifted her hand toward the circle. "Please, join us for the circle."

"All right, everyone!" Jo raised her arms to draw everyone's attention. "We've come to celebrate the year of the stag. This will be a year of regeneration, leadership, wisdom, and experience." She looked from one person to the next and paused on Autumn. "So much happened this past year. We've lost loved ones and reclaimed some. We've discovered new facets of ourselves and the courage to take up our destinies. And now . . . it is time to become stronger than we have ever been before. To lead with our hearts and minds as one, establishing our new four-points coven and pulling from the past to expand in the future. So with the spark of our bonfire this evening, may we prosper in the new year!"

Giving her aunt a warm hug, Autumn stepped forward and beckoned Lainy to do the same. Tavish circled between their feet as Autumn addressed the group next.

"Jo is right. This past year has brought so many lessons. I've stepped out of my comfort zone and learned to be confident and strong even in the face of things I never could have imagined. And in the process, I realized I was never alone. You all always stood by my side." Autumn rubbed her palms together and blew a breath into them as she nodded to Lainy beside her. "So in the year of the stag, it's our time to lead the mountain region into a new era of balance and harmony." She and Lainy opened their palms and lifted them to the sky in unison. "And it's time to rekindle our strength!"

Flames burst from the firewood in the center of the circle and rose high as everyone watched in awe of the girls' fire abilities. Autumn and Lainy exchanged a smile and stepped closer to the bonfire.

"Now, everyone, please enjoy the fire and good company," Penny said over the dull chatting of everyone around the circle. "When you're ready, Autumn and Simone have brought us some new year fortunes from their shop." She lifted a wicker basket lined with flannel fabric and filled with bright-red rolled papers twisted at the ends. "You're welcome to take a prediction and tie it to a pine tree to anchor your good fortune."

James grabbed a flannel blanket lying on a large log and walked over to Autumn. He wrapped the blanket around them both and faced her. "I don't know if I have enough water within me to keep up with all that's inside of you, but I'm willing to try."

She snuggled in close to him and looked up into his warm eyes. "Who said anything about keeping up? I'll always be beside you, no matter what. Come hurricane winds or raging fires, I still want and need your calm waters." Autumn lifted her chin to kiss his lips as he pulled her in even tighter with the blanket.

"I guess I'll be the first to hang my fortune on the tree," Eve called as she turned to head toward the trees encircling the clearing. She took a few steps away from the bonfire and stopped in her tracks, gasping at something in front of her.

Tavish perked up from his place beside the bonfire and looked out at the tree line by Eve, signaling Autumn to do the same.

"Eve?" Penny stood from her place on a large log to see what had startled the girl. "Oh my word."

A substantially built stag with massive antlers stood directly in front of Eve between a few pine trees. He shook a bit of snow from his antlers and took a few steps toward her until his eyes met hers. Everyone around the bonfire stopped in silence to watch the interaction.

Eve swallowed hard and whispered under her breath, "Strength and experience." She reached out a hand and placed it gently on the stag's nose.

The animal closed his eyes as several more deer appeared in the background of the forest. When he opened them again, the stag moved to the side and scraped his front hoof along the ground several times. Bowing his head at the group, he then turned and trotted off into the forest with the rest of the deer.

With her heart pounding, Eve put her hands on her chest and turned toward the bonfire. Her mouth dropped open as she met eyes with everyone staring at her. "Did you all see that?"

Autumn, Simone, and Lainy walked up to meet her. They each put their hands on her to make sure she was all right.

"That was pretty incredible. You just locked eyes with the head buck." Simone widened her eyes at Eve. "Pretty brave for a small-town baker."

Laughing under her breath at her cousin, Autumn met Eve's eyes. "Seriously, though, are you okay? That was intense!"

With a sigh, Eve nodded hesitantly. "Yeah, I'm good, actually. I mean, that was totally surreal, but it was also a complete rush! When I touched its nose, I felt its power rushing through me, almost like a massive freight train. But, I mean, it was a calm and stable freight train. Does that make sense?"

Penny stepped forward to join the girls. "The stag has immense power. The animal wanted you to feel its presence and connection to it. That's why it marked the ground here." She pointed to the side where the stag had dragged its hoof along the ground.

Autumn walked over and knelt to place a hand over the spot the stag had scraped. "I sense it, too. There's power in this place. It's been here all along, but it's like . . . the stag enhanced it for us."

"And the fire grew larger as well." Lainy pointed behind them. "Look. The wood within the fire started burning with a deeper shade of red."

"All elements become one," Jo chimed in.

"Maybe this is a good time for our refreshments," Penny suggested. "Autumn, dear, would you help me gather them at the cottage?"

Autumn nodded. "Sure, Mom. Good idea." Tavish followed as Autumn and her mother walked together down the dirt path through the sanctuary woods toward Hawthorn Cottage. They linked arms and enjoyed the breeze flowing gently through the trees on either side of them.

When they reached the opening at Gran's old cottage, something caught Autumn's eye on the opposite side. "The wisps," she said aloud.

"Wisps? Are you sure?" Penny replied.

Walking slowly across the front of the property toward the woods by Mrs. Pendleton's house, a tiny blue-sapphire light popped out from the forest floor.

"There it is again." Autumn quickened her pace as her mother followed.

"Wait, Autumn!" Penny called, but stopped in her tracks as two people moved out of the tree line. She dropped to her knees as tears formed in her eyes. Covering her mouth in her hand, she said the name she never expected to say again. "Laith."

CHAPTER 28

Mrs. Pendleton prodded Laith forward toward Autumn and Penny. His stature shined with lavender shimmers surrounding him, and he looked like he had barely aged more than a couple years. Autumn eyed him curiously as her mother came up beside her.

"I imagined the worst since it had been so long." Penny wiped the tears from her eyes.

Laith smiled and brushed the back of his hand across Penny's cheek. "But you knew deep down that I would return."

"I hoped, yes. But the way we left things . . ." Penny shook her head and turned to Autumn. "Oh, now . . . There's someone you should meet."

"Ah, yes! We have met on occasion, just not in the proper sense." Laith stood in front of Autumn and looked her up and down. "I've waited for this moment for a very long time."

"Autumn, dear," Mrs. Pendleton interjected. "This is your father and my nephew, Laith."

Staring into his hazel eyes, Autumn felt as though she were looking into a mirror. All at once, she caught glimpses of her childhood when she'd played with ladybugs and spotted sapphire lights in the woods.

"What do you mean, we've met on occasion?" She watched the lavender shimmers bouncing off his skin, and the trail of wisps dancing around his feet.

Laith looked down at his feet. "Wisps are a curious energy, don't you think?" He bent down and moved his hands between the wisps to catch them like fireflies. "They hold the same resonance as the fae. We are predominantly earth energies, after all. And I presume you know that the ancestral tree holds our doorway." He looked back toward the woods near Mrs. Pendleton's house. "Your mother has always called to me through her dreams. After I left, I sensed your connection between us, but it was still too dangerous for me to leave my land. So, I sent the wisps with my energy. Over time, though, I needed to know more about you."

"That's when we decided I should come." Mrs. Pendleton gave Laith a pat on the shoulder. "While Laith and my sister carried the responsibility of defending our land in tumultuous times, I did not have that burden. So, I knew my place lay here with you, and I was privileged to watch you grow all these years."

"Oh, my!" Penny rested her hands over her heart to calm the emotions she felt. "All this time, I had no idea! Why didn't you tell me?"

Mrs. Pendleton gave her a warm smile. "It was for the best, love. Autumn and I discussed it already, but she needed to grow with the support of the witches around her. Your mother, Lorna, found out over the years, but she waited for the right time to reveal the truth."

"So you both waited all these years." Autumn shook her head. "And what do we do now?"

"Why, you get to know each other, of course!" Mrs. Pendleton laughed. "And please, no more of this Mrs. Pendleton business. Remember, you can call me Freya when it's just us."

Laith smiled at his aunt and nodded. "Freya longed for this day just as I have, but I mustn't stay. Today is only the beginning for us, though. And from now on, you know you can connect with me through the wisps."

Autumn thought for a moment. "The portal opening is dwindling again, isn't it?"

"Yes, I'm afraid it is." Freya looked back into the woods. "This may be our only chance for a while, but I wanted you to meet."

"Freya." Autumn grasped at her locket and ran her fingers over the tree root emblem on it. "This is why I never see you in town, isn't it? The bell that affects me also affects you."

Penny gasped at the thought. "The iron bell. Oh, Freya, all these years!"

"It's all right, really. The gift of seeing you every day far outweighed the limitations of my whereabouts." Freya laughed. "Besides, you know I love being a homebody."

"Well, maybe we can help with that." Autumn turned to her mother and exchanged a glance.

"Mmmm, I think you're right, my little ladybug. Come, we have a job to do." Penny led them all past Gran's cottage and into the sanctuary woods on the opposite side of the house. Laith trod so lightly on the dirt that he made no footprints as he walked.

When they approached the clearing, everyone stopped chatting to stare at Laith and Freya. The trees grew quiet, and only the sound of the crackling bonfire continued.

Autumn stepped forward and cleared her throat. "Everyone, I'd like you to meet two very special people. This is my great aunt Freya and my father, Laith."

Jo's mouth dropped open, and she scurried up to meet them. "Good sky above, it's about time! Freya . . . I thought you'd never reveal yourself." She turned to Laith and wrapped her arms around him. "And Laith, my sister can finally find the peace she deserves."

"We need everyone's help," Autumn continued. "In case you can't tell by the shimmers, the three of us have fae blood."

Ayla gasped and stumbled back a few steps. "No," she whispered under her breath. She shoved her hand into her coat pocket and pulled out a small thimble, holding it up high in front of her. Sorcha and Dillon grabbed her arms and held her tightly to calm her down.

Autumn saw a glint on the iron thimble's surface and immediately called upon the winds. A white mountain owl swooped down from the treetops and hooked its claws over the thimble within Ayla's hand. It soared high with the thimble to a branch on a large pine tree.

Sobbing in her siblings' arms, Ayla collapsed on the ground. "No more fae, please."

Laith softly walked up to her as the shimmers around him changed to a lighter green color. "I sense that the dark fae have hurt you." He took Ayla's hands in his as she shook uncontrollably. "We are not the Unseelie people who have harmed you before. I can see that you are a dream walker as I am. You have the strength of the waters within you, and now . . ." He paused to send a brilliant green light into Ayla's hands. "You also have the safety of the earth in your heart. Do not fear, for as you dream and move through worlds, you shall from now on be safe."

Closing his eyes, Laith summoned the energy of the earth within him. He spoke in a deep, clear tone. "Through the stability of the earth, the strength of the light fae converges with your water spirit. All the days and in worlds beyond, as above and so below."

He opened his eyes to find Ayla looking at him in awe. She removed her hands from his and flipped them over to watch the green shimmers within them. Her eyes met Laith's, and she wrapped her arms around him. "For the first time since that dark woman took me, I feel safe. Thank you."

"Well, now"—Penny put her hands on her hips and gave Autumn a look—"I actually could use that thimble to perform the spell. Any chance we could get it back?"

Autumn raised her head to the treetops and sighed. "Yeah, sorry, it was kind of a knee-jerk reaction. Let me see what I can do." She focused her energy on the white owl and called to it in her mind. "We appreciate your support, and now you can return the object to the circle." She raised her arms toward the pine tree and let the winds flow through the trees.

A moment later, the white owl returned and dropped the thimble down directly between Penny and the bonfire. Smiling with appreciation, Penny drew a circle around the thimble in the dirt.

"Very well, thank you, Autumn." Penny cleared her throat and looked around the clearing at everyone. "Now, as Autumn was saying, we need everyone's help. The iron bell at city hall is dangerous to the fae, including those here whom we love. Since my late mother's cloaking spell dissipated with her passing, the time has come to renew it once again."

Jo stepped forward to stand beside her sister at the fire. "The thimble shall serve as a totem for the iron bell. Autumn, Laith, and Freya, stand at the opening to the clearing so as not to get too close. We shall initiate the spell around the bonfire."

"Good, now please come forward and link hands." Penny waved them all toward the fire. "Focus your intention on setting a boundary around the iron bell in town. We will create this spell to block all harmful effects to these three alone. Simone and Eve, since you two have proven to be strong magical companions through this whole escapade, I'd like you to work the spell."

"Us?" Simone pointed her fingers to her chest and then back at Eve. "You want us to activate it?"

"Your aunt is right, dear," Jo said sincerely to her daughter. "The spell will hold much longer if the next generation performs it, and you've both proven yourselves to be more than capable."

Simone sighed and gave a quick nod to Eve. "All right, you set the boundary while I work the spell as part of the circle."

Eve moved toward Penny in front of the thimble on the ground. She bent down and placed her hands on either side of the dirt circle Penny had drawn. Taking a deep breath to calm her energy, she lifted her gaze to Simone. "Okay, I'm ready."

Locking hands tightly with her mother, Simone closed her eyes, and everyone else followed around the bonfire. She blew out a deep breath and began the spell.

"Rain of the earth, I call upon you. As this thimble lay forged in iron, so, too, does the bell of Hollow's Glenn," Simone continued as Eve moved her right hand in a clockwise motion around the thimble. "Wash over the bell and cloak it to be unseen. May no negative effects befall these fae three. As above, so below. Create this cloak as I deem it so."

Small droplets fell onto Eve's hand as she made one last circle. She looked up to the sky as the drops grew larger and fell directly into the dirt circle. Scooting back on the ground, she allowed the drops to form a pool within the boundary on the earth.

Simone replaced her hands in the chain with those beside her and walked over to where Eve knelt. She eyed the pool of water with the thimble in the center and remarked to Eve, "I think we've done it."

Eve smiled broadly and nodded. "Yeah, I think we did!"

Kneeling beside her coven sister, Simone took Eve's hand and stared into the pool of water. "Seal this spell with the energy and strength of the four-points. Earth, air, fire, and water. With my words, let none supersede or over this boundary impede."

Taking a breath, the girls released hands as Autumn walked up behind them. "I can feel the boundary in place again. You did it." She wrapped her arms through each of theirs. "And such an unlikely pair, earth and water." Smirking at Simone, Autumn nodded in thanks.

Simone rolled her eyes. "Yeah, well, there's definitely something good to that earth energy when it produces such amazing pastries all the time."

"Oh, the refreshments!" Eve dropped their arms and ran back down the tree-lined path toward the cottage, with Tavish galloping close behind her.

"Looks like someone's expecting his favorite treats," Jo remarked before enveloping Simone and Autumn in a big hug. "I'm proud of you, girls. And if that stag gave us any indication, I expect this year to be our best one yet."

Chapter 29

Autumn flipped the lights on in the back room of Parchment and Pine and dropped Tavish's basket to the ground. The cat jumped out and immediately headed for the front door of the shop.

"Tav, where are you headed? We haven't even started the fire yet." Autumn shook her head at the cat and hung her coat and backpack up on a hook.

"It seems we already have a visitor," Simone said with a groan. "Do I have to unlock the door?"

Autumn peeked out from the back, confused. She squinted to see Anabeth Greenwood peering in the front window at Tavish. She knocked on the window and pointed to the front door.

"Would you stop?" Autumn rolled her eyes at her cousin as she walked toward the front door. "Anabeth has been helpful, and she's a friend now. Of course we're going to open the door."

Sighing, Simone sat down behind the computer at the back counter. "If you insist."

Pulling the front door open, Autumn greeted Anabeth with a smile. "Morning."

Anabeth pushed straight inside with her intern, Finn, right behind her. She had a concerned look on her face that told Autumn she was a bit off her game from the usual straight-faced Anabeth she knew.

"Did you say 'good morning' or just 'morning'?" Anabeth waved her hand in the air. "Whatever, let's just keep it at 'morning,' because that's what it is."

"I actually wanted to ask you about the Philip Gibson case, so I'm glad you're here." Autumn walked up beside Anabeth as she stared out the front window. "Did the paper run the final story about his death?"

"Oh yeah, the police labeled it an accident in the end." Anabeth continued eyeing the street outside. "Something about him hitting his head on the rocky cliffs in the dark. The police said that a fall caused his death, and no evidence substantiated any foul play, so that was that."

Autumn looked back at Simone and exchanged a telepathic thought that the evidence had disappeared into the portal.

Keeping quiet, she turned her focus back to Anabeth. "Well, I'm glad the police wrapped everything up."

Anabeth pursed her lips and stared at Autumn for a moment. "I'm here about another . . . situation."

Simone jumped up from the computer and crossed her arms. "Are we talking about an 'in trouble with the law' type of situation or just an 'I can't find my car keys' situation?"

Finn perused the shop tables and picked up a few journals before interjecting. "It's more of a 'dead relative and arson' situation."

"Oh!" Autumn scooped up the cat into her arms and waved them all into the hearth room. "We better put the fire on, then."

"And some darjeeling tea, I'm thinking." Simone shook her pointer finger in the air as she headed to the back room. "Be back in a sec."

Autumn threw a few logs into the fireplace as Anabeth settled into one of the wingback chairs in the hearth room. The fire sparked after just a few seconds and put their guest at ease for a moment.

Anabeth stared into the fire and crossed her legs before shaking her foot furiously as she thought about why she came into the shop. "Not sure if you've heard yet, but there's been an explosion at the university science lab. They're calling it an accident for now, but I've been around the block long enough to know they're not saying something. It was arson."

"Okay, and you don't think the police handled it well?" Autumn looked between Anabeth and Finn in confusion.

"Her cousin worked at the lab and died in the fire." Finn took the direct route to give Autumn more details. "The police notified their family last night, and now our editor's not letting Anabeth investigate the story. Too close to it, he said."

"I'm sorry, Anabeth. That must be hard." Autumn sat down in the other wingback chair across the round table from Anabeth. "What is it you need from us?"

Simone walked in with a tray of teacups and set it down on the table. "Whoa, your aura is all over the place today." She eyed Anabeth with wide eyes.

Anabeth stopped shaking her foot and took a teacup. "That's exactly why I need your help. My cousin and I were very close, and she mentioned to me a couple times that the lab manager seemed shady. Not in the usual sense, but in the . . ."—Anabeth looked behind her at Finn for a moment, wondering if she should continue. Lowering her voice a bit, she leaned in toward Autumn and Simone—"the shadowy magic kind of sense."

Autumn watched the edge of Finn's mouth draw up in a slight smile at the mention of magic. "Anabeth, I'll be blunt with you because I know you can handle it." Autumn sighed and stared at Finn. "Finn is an air witch like me." Finn squirmed a little as Autumn said it out loud.

"Oh, please," Simone said as she gave him a teacup. "Anabeth knows about us, and every witch in town sees the magic written all over you. You're not fooling anyone here in Hollow's Glenn."

"From what I know," Autumn continued, "an earth witch heads up the science department at the university. I only know because my mother used to work in the holistic medicine department up there. So your cousin probably just sensed the earth magic around the lab."

Anabeth shook her head and put her teacup down. She pressed her pointer finger down hard on the table. "No, I don't buy it. My cousin may not have been magical like the rest of you . . ."—she turned toward Finn and looked him up and down—"but she certainly was intuitive. And if she thought something was going on, then something was going on." Anabeth pulled her phone out of her coat pocket and scrolled through her messages. "Plus, she told me before she died she found something in the manager's office. And early yesterday evening, before the fire happened, she texted me this picture." She lifted her phone to show the girls a photo of wrinkled graph paper with old symbols, letters, and numbers written into formulas.

Autumn and Simone exchanged a serious glance before Simone turned to loosen the ties on the curtains around the hearth room archway.

"How much do you all know about ancient alchemy?" Finn asked.

"Enough," Autumn said. "And if that's what this is, then you're right. This was no accident, and someone is playing with fire."

Next In Series

Get the next book in the Hollow's Glenn Coven Mystery Series!

An Inferno of Ire, book 4 in the series, is available at the link below.

A mysterious and deadly fire at the university laboratory suggests a dangerous ancient alchemy at work. Will the coven be able to decipher who's playing with fire before the one responsible brings Hollow's Glenn to a tragic end?

Don't miss another mesmerizing story with your favorite characters from Hollow's Glenn!

Grab your copy now!

https://kristenkingwrites.com/hollowsglennseries

**Download your FREE Prequel Novella
to the
Hollow's Glenn Coven Mystery Series,**

A Land Of Consequence.

Find out Autumn's origin story and what kept her mother,
Penny, in the mountain region for so many years.
Go to:

https://dl.bookfunnel.com/azstlfr1se
To get your copy now!

A Note From The Author

Thank you so much for reading my cozy paranormal mystery, *An Eclipse of Evidence*. I hope the characters spoke to you and that you fell in love with the inviting mountain town of Hollow's Glenn. If you'd like to share the enjoyment with fellow readers, then leaving an online book review would support those interested in cozy reads as well. That way, we can create a movement of magical readers in love with the worlds and possibilities in each story.

Now, as this book is part of the Hollow's Glenn Coven Mystery series, there will be more opportunities to get immersed in the world of the MacKinnon girls and the founding families. Plus, with each book, I'll share some practical magic such as Gran's tea recipes, Autumn's seasonal journaling prompts, and Eve's pastry recipes.

You can also hop onto my newsletter list to get the prequel with Penny's story of how she left for the mountain region and why she stayed so long. You may even find out how Autumn's gifts started.

To read the free prequel novella, *A Land of Consequence*, and hear about the latest releases and other goodies, scan here:

Acknowledgments

This book is for all the creative souls longing to pour their hearts into what inspires them. May you always push the boundaries of this world and explore the depths of your imaginative spirit to show others new ways of perceiving our reality and beyond.

About The Author

Kristen is an Amazon best-selling author, spiritual life coach, and creative. After many years blending project management, design, and coaching, she now lets her water energy lead the way through creative fiction writing. She finds that a good dose of magic sets the coziest tone for any day.

When not channeling her inner writing muse, Kristen enjoys baking for her family, creating herbal concoctions, and tapping into all things metaphysical. She spends time snuggling in her mountain home next to a cozy fire and her calico cat, with plenty of candles and jazz playing softly in the background. She loves to lose herself taking photos, pulling tarot cards, or charging crystals by the light of the moon.

For more from the author and to find her books and offerings, go to:

https://www.kristenkingwrites.com